MY   326381
                             13.95
Flynn   May/985
Murder on the Hudson

DATE DUE			

MURDER ON THE HUDSON

Also by Don Flynn

Murder Isn't Enough

MURDER ON THE HUDSON

Don Flynn

Walker and Company
New York

All the characters and events portrayed in this story
are fictitious.

First published in the United States of America
in 1985 by the Walker Publishing Company, Inc.

Published simultaneously in Canada by John Wiley & Sons
Canada, Limited, Rexdale, Ontario.

Library of Congress Cataloging in Publication Data

Flynn, Don.
    Murder on the Hudson.

    I. Title.
PS3556.L84M84   1985   813'.54   84-17306
ISBN: 0–8027–5609–3

Printed in the United States of America

Book design by Teresa M. Carboni

10   9   8   7   6   5   4   3   2   1

For Kevin, Christopher, and Colin
Who made this book necessary

DEATH SHOULD BE AWAITED "with a cheerful mind, since it is nothing but the dissolving of the elements of which each living thing is composed," advises the wise Roman emperor Marcus Aurelius. "You have taken ship, you have made the voyage; you have come to port; disembark."

The Aurelian maxim was in my head that morning as I stood on the cafeteria deck in the stern of the Hudson River Cruises excursion boat staring down at the inert form that had "joined the majority." Marcus was correct, as usual. The middle-aged man with the fringe of beard around his chin was the one least concerned about his departure. He cared not at all that his sudden demise had scrubbed the cruiser's usual day-long excursion trip up the Hudson River to Bear Mountain and Hyde Park and back.

My city editor at the New York *Daily Press*, Ironhead Matthews, had sent me to have a look when it came over the police radio that the cruiser had turned around at the George Washington Bridge and was returning to its pier at Forty-first Street.

Detective Jim Lawler of the Tenth Precinct was squatting beside the body examining his papers when I walked up.

"Who is he?" I asked.

"ID says Howard Ritter. Looks about forty-eight."

"Anything else on him?"

Lawler was shuffling papers and cards. "What's this? He's got an Actors Equity card."

"He's an actor?"

"He's got a card, Fitzgerald. That's all I'm saying. That is, *if* this is Howard Ritter to begin with. There's no positive ID till somebody identifies him."

That's the way it is with cops and dead bodies. They don't want to tell you anything positively or officially until somebody tells *them* something positively and officially. Cops, to tell the truth, don't know anything except what they're told. They're as bad as newspapermen.

Big Jim Lawler stood up. He's six-three with reddish hair and tired eyes. "Who found him?" he wanted to know.

A middle-aged black lady named Mrs. Phillips who was shepherding four young kids was brought forward, and she said she was the one.

"He was jes' sittin' there in the booth by the back window," she said. "An' all of a sudden he was dead."

"You didn't see anything?"

"No, sir. There he sat. We thought he was asleep. Didn't say nuthin'. Sittin' there holdin' his belly."

Mrs. Phillips thought the old man had "had a accident" when she saw the drippings falling from the booth onto the floor. "Then I saw the drops was all red."

No one had heard a shot. No one had seen anything. All that was certain was that a middle-aged man was sitting in a booth in the cafeteria of the excursion boat with a bullet in his stomach. The assistant medical examiner said later that the slug had probably been fired from very close and had ripped through the man's stomach, liver, and kidneys. He may have been standing up and then sunk down into the booth. The shot apparently was muffled enough so that no one heard it.

You might think that if a person was shot to death in the company of more than a thousand other people in broad daylight, there would be nothing much left to do but to remove

2

the body to the morgue and the killer to The Tombs. Except that on this particular occasion, nobody seemed to know who the killer was.

Anyway, it wasn't long before a young woman was led onto the boat and back toward the stern. She was staring fixedly at the lump under a brown quilted blanket on the cafeteria floor, and even as she came forward she was trying to lean backward. Her pretty red mouth was moving, muttering and chirping things I couldn't make out that were probably "Oh, my God!" and "Oh, no!"

She was, it turned out, Jennifer Ritter, Howard's daughter, who lived with him down near Gramercy Park. She had been driven to the pier in a squad car. She looked as pale as a mannequin in a Bloomingdale's window.

When she had been shoved up, more or less, close enough, the assistant medical examiner knelt down and lifted the blanket so she could see the dead man's face.

"Uhhhhhhhhhh!" Jennifer gasped, and turned away.

"I'm sorry, Miss," Detective Lawler said in his official Police Department voice. "Can you identify him?"

Jennifer nodded her head but said nothing and didn't look again.

"Is it Howard Ritter, your father?"

Jennifer nodded again and murmured, "It is." And then the tears came.

Howard Ritter had been an actor, all right. Not Richard Burton, you understand, but an actor, all his life. When I checked the news library later, we had only a few clips about him. He had done pretty well for a while as Grandpa Vanderhof in a revival of *You Can't Take It With You*, but other than that his entire acting career apparently had been playing the Muleteer in *Man of La Mancha* in various companies. Life is like that for some stage actors. They play almost exclusively the same role during their entire professional career, like Yul Brynner, who was just about irrevocably typed by *The King and I.* Or sometimes they can't get any other part because there are so few acting jobs, or maybe both.

Lawler's partner, a young detective named Rocco Santelli, set up a little table beside the gangplank. As the boat passengers filed off, Detective Santelli took down their names and checked their identifications. Somebody among the more than one thousand passengers apparently had shot and killed Howard Ritter. Lawler watched the shuffling procession, and I don't think I ever saw a man look so frustrated.

"Damn," he muttered, "a thousand suspects."

"But hell, Lawless, sometimes you don't have *any*."

"What's the difference?" Lawler glared at me.

A squad car had been pulled up on the pier and I spotted a cop in the back seat with a hand-held movie camera discreetly taking pictures of the passengers as they came off.

Reporters are supposed to be callous brutes who think nothing of questioning rape victims, but that's a lot of crap. I've always felt embarrassed asking questions of people whose parent, child, or loved one has been murdered. I remember once I had to interview a policeman who had undergone a sex change operation and had become a "policewoman." Felt like a damned idiot. But no matter how you feel, you still have to do it. I moved over to Jennifer Ritter.

"What was your father doing on the boat?"

"What?" she said, standing at the rail, trying to concentrate. "Oh. Uh . . . let me think . . . I don't know. He went out to deliver something."

"To the riverboat?"

"He didn't tell me where."

"What was he delivering?"

"I don't know."

"Who was he taking it to?"

"Are you a policeman?"

"No, ma'am. Edward Fitzgerald, *Daily Press*."

She could have been an actress herself, with her looks. She wore a yellow sundress and her legs and arms were the kind of tan you associate with the Hamptons, even though I've never been to the Hamptons. The top was cut low enough to catch my attention, and her neck was a stately column leading to a lovely head with hair the color of India ink. Her face was all huge brown eyes and red mouth, animated at the moment with anxiety and concern.

"Am I allowed to talk to you?"

"Well, a story might help get this cleared up."

Jennifer Ritter blinked and dabbed at her eyes. She was a twitching mobile. "I don't know, Mr. Fitzgerald. Somebody called about a job delivering something, and he did it. Actors take any job that comes along, you know."

"Uh-huh."

It was all very informative. Howard Ritter the actor got a job from somebody she didn't know to deliver something she couldn't identify to an unknown destination and ended up dead on the Hudson River. Crystal clear.

"Drugs, maybe?"

Jennifer Ritter's eyes suddenly became focused and intent. She glared at me with a flushed, angry face. "What do you mean?"

"Nothing. Just trying out possibilities. He must have been delivering something."

"Well, not drugs!" She took a couple of steps away, and it was as though she had moved a mile. I followed.

"Okay, okay. Just asking."

"It might have been wine."

"What kind of wine?"

"I don't think I'm supposed to talk to you." She strode past me and tugged at Detective Lawler's arm. "Am I supposed to talk to this reporter?"

Lawler turned as though noticing me for the first time.

"Absolutely not, Miss," he said, and glared at me. "Fitzgerald, you know you're not supposed to talk to her."

"Okay, okay," I said, knowing he was just saying it for the daughter's benefit.

She spun and punctured me with those relentless brown eyes again.

The interview was over; that was obvious. I walked toward the middle of the boat again, where Santelli sat watching the passengers straggling down the gangplank.

"What are you doing? You've got no right to take my name." A red-faced, pugnacious man had reached the little table and Officer Santelli, and now he was backing off and protesting. Lawler came over. "You in charge here, officer?" the guy asked Lawler.

"That's right. What's the trouble?"

"I don't know anything about this. You have no probable cause to stop me," the excited man said with a mixture of anger and worry. He had a bushy moustache and a helmet of tight curls like the wig of a minister at the court of Louis XV.

"A crime has been committed on this boat, Mister," said Lawler patiently. I noticed a slim woman in lavender slacks and a yellow top moving over behind the protesting man. She kept looking away from Lawler.

The tall detective sighed when he heard the words "probable cause." The man had to be a lawyer.

"I'm not identifying myself, and neither is my companion," the man said defiantly, backing against the boat rail and standing there stiffly.

"All right, all right, stand over there," Lawler said disgustedly. "Keep the line moving there."

"Are you detaining us?" the man challenged.

"That's right," said Lawler. "You don't want to give me your name, you can give it to the district attorney."

"Oh, my God," sniffled the lavender slacks, but the man shushed her and told her it would be "all right—they can't push people around."

"They under arrest?" I asked Lawler. He made a face and looked away. He wanted me there about as much as a South Bronx aficionado at a cockfight would want a uniformed cop in the place.

"No," he sighed.

"You holding them?"

"Hey, Fitz," he pleaded, "don't ya see I'm busy? How do I know if I'm holding them? Later, huh?"

I left. Lawler had his hands full if the guy was a lawyer and really knew about "probable cause," which is a nice legal phrase that means you can't stop a person unless you personally see him shoot somebody and you've got a reliable witness to back you up. "Probable cause" means somebody looks suspicious, but at the same time it says there's no such thing as looking suspicious. Don't even ask me. It's one of those U.S. Supreme Court decisions that make cops helpless.

Back at my electronic video display terminal in the *Daily Press* city room, I wrote a screen about Ritter, and we ran a picture of him sprawled on the deck of the boat. There was also a little head shot of him in the corner of the larger photo. So Ritter exited in character, his last role that of a dead body in the stern of a riverboat.

I checked with Detective Lawler by phone later at the Tenth Precinct about all those wonderful suspects—turned out there were 1,412—and asked about the guy who wouldn't give his name.

"What can I tell you?" he said with an edge. "Had to let him go without identifying him. There was no probable cause to detain him."

"Did you get his picture anyway?"

There was a silence, and then I heard his breath come out. "Aw, Jesus. Look, never mind the pictures, huh?"

"Okay, Lawless. You'll let me know if anything turns up on the other fourteen hundred suspects?"

"Yeah, yeah."

"Got a tail on that lawyer?"

"So long, Fitz."

I hung up. I pretty much forgot about it after that. Murders are nothing unusual in New York City, even murders of actors, especially obscure ones. A day later the phone rang at my desk in the city room, and it was Jennifer Ritter, that whimpering, bereaved daughter. She wasn't whimpering this time, though.

"Say, Mr. Fitzgerald, this is Jenny Ritter. You remember me?"

"Sure," I said, her red mouth and lovely face swimming up before me.

"Listen, I'm sorry I was so bitchy the other day. I was really half crazy."

"I know."

"Have you heard any more about my father's case?"

"Well, no."

"Do they have any leads yet? I can never reach that detective."

I sighed. It does no good to tell people that detectives of the New York City Police Department are not out trying to solve murders. People think cops actually go out and work on cases. They do, for about twenty-four hours—sometimes forty-eight hours. After that, if the case isn't solved and it isn't at least murder at the Waldorf-Astoria or the Metropolitan Opera, they move on to the next. And there are always next ones. A homicide detective and his partner will have forty or fifty unsolved murders in their file. So unless leads keep developing or the case has priority, a homicide detective is forced to put it aside after a couple of days. Then it depends upon a break. If nothing new turns up, the case may lie there unsolved forever. The cops don't like to admit any cases are dormant, but they are.

"I haven't heard any more," I said. Which was true.

"Are you going to write another story?"

That was another thing. People think a newspaper is interested in writing story after story about something even though nothing new has happened. What do you write after the first story: "Howard Ritter, the actor, was still dead yesterday"?

"Not unless something develops," I said, which is a dodge

reporters use to get rid of callers when they don't know what else to do.

"You said a story might help solve this," she said.

Yes, I had said that, but we had already printed a story, I explained.

"You mean that's *it*? The story's dead?"

"Unless something happens."

"Oh . . ."

I told her the unhappy facts of life about murder in New York, which is that it's so commonplace that very few homicides can hold headlines long. I could hear her breath go out. She grunted with disgust. I didn't blame her.

"What a city," she said, not really to anyone.

"Yeah."

Then she started again, and I could see those dark, intent eyes. "But you'll do what you can, won't you?" she pleaded. "I've seen your by-line in the paper . . . you have some clout, don't you?"

What could I say? It's funny the way a reporter's clout is obvious to everyone except the reporter.

I probably would never have seen her again if she hadn't called once more a couple of days later.

"Ed Fitzgerald?" she said in a quick, breathless voice.

"What? Who is this?"

"It's me—Jenny Ritter! Listen, they came to my house!"

"Who did?"

"I don't know. Some man. He threatened me!"

"What do you mean? Why?"

"Eddie, I'm terrified! He told me he wants the money back that my father stole."

9

2

JENNIFER RITTER LIVED IN an apartment down on Irving Place just below Gramercy Park, a rent-stabilized place that her father had managed to get during one of his flush periods.

"Who is it?" she called out when I rang the bell.

"It's me," I said. "Ed Fitzgerald . . . *Daily Press.*" Pretty formal, but then she was clearly taking no chances on allowing any more infiltrators past the bunker on the Maginot Line.

I could sense her peeking out at me through the thick, glassplug peephole, and then the locks started opening and clanking like chains on a watertight door in the bulkhead of a battleship. When the last one clanked, the door flew open, and she rushed out, almost dashing into me.

"Mr. Fitzgerald," she said, and she was trembling.

"Hey," I said, "take it easy."

She glanced up and down the hall. "Let's get out of here," she told me, and led me to the elevator. As we waited, she kept looking back and forth like a cat in a cage, and there was no sense in trying to get anything out of her then.

We walked outside and down Irving Place to a nice old bar—Pete's Tavern—where O. Henry used to write short stories in the booths. They've still got one from *The New York World Magazine* framed under glass on the wall. And there's a sign next to it:

"In this booth O. Henry wrote 'The Gift of the Magi' in the year 1905."

Anyway, as soon as we were safely inside and in a booth, she relaxed a little and let out a long, deep breath.

"My God, I was scared to death," she blurted out. "Eddie, he said I've got to give him fifty thousand dollars!"

"Wait, Jennifer. Who said that?"

Her enormous eyes searched my face anxiously. "I don't know. I never saw him before."

All she knew was that a large, dark-skinned man with black hair was waiting for her when she got off the elevator, and that he had shoved her roughly into her apartment when she opened the door.

"I didn't know what to think," she said.

The large, dark-haired man had immediately assured her that he was not there to harm her, but only to get his money back.

"I asked him, 'What money?' and he said, 'You know what money. The money Ritter took from me.'"

The man had searched the apartment frenetically, turning drawers upside down and going through papers like a cyclone. He apparently did not find what he was looking for.

The waiter brought her a white wine and me a Schaefer, and we sipped them for a moment. I was trying to figure out what it could mean.

"That's all he said? He wanted fifty thousand dollars that your father had stolen?"

"That's it! Eddie, my father wouldn't steal a penny from a fountain."

I looked at her beseeching face, which was locked in eye contact with me. She was silently, desperately begging for an answer.

Things might have been a lot easier if she were a little less anxious and vulnerable and attractive and if Belinda Sharpe had not gone home to Wales and left me alone in my apartment on East Eighty-second Street. I tried to look knowing,

12

but of course I hadn't a clue. I had thought the story would dribble away, the murder probably being the work of one of the heartless dingos that roam the Big Apple looking for easy prey. Now it was clear that it would not go away.

"Jennifer, you have to figure out what he was doing. Why did somebody kill him?"

Jennifer's great eyes closed, squeezing out tears, and she shook her bowed head energetically back and forth.

"There was no reason, Ed. None."

There was never any reason, naturally, until you could find it.

"Listen, you said he went out on an errand that day. To deliver something. Maybe wine."

"Yes," she said, looking up.

"You don't know for sure?"

"He said it was wine. There was a man who used to call him and ask him to bring cold wine to him."

"Bring it where?"

Jennifer searched her memory. "Different places. Once he went to Central Park when the Philharmonic was playing. And he went to the top of the World Trade Center once."

"Who was this man? Do you know?"

"Goodman," she said, remembering. "Daddy said a Mr. Goodman."

"You think he was delivering wine to this Mr. Goodman on the boat?"

"I don't know. It's a short trip for two hundred dollars."

"What two hundred dollars?"

"That's what the guy paid him."

It's funny the way people who are excited think you know things you don't know. "How do you know he was paid two hundred dollars?" I asked.

"Because that's what he was paid the time before that."

"He got two hundred each time?" I asked.

Jennifer shook her head. "No, no. It was a hundred the first couple of times. Then the last couple of times it was two."

"For delivering bottles of wine?" I'm afraid there was newspaperman cynicism in my voice.

"Yes!" she said anxiously. "I know it sounds funny. Daddy said he was a rich old guy, and he wanted a confidential messenger. That's why he paid so well."

I looked at her. "Maybe there was something else in those packages."

Her tear-stained face appeared from between her hands again. "Don't you dare tell me drugs!"

"I'm not. But it must have been something worth money. He was being paid plenty. *How* was he paid?"

"He would get half of it in advance and half afterward."

"Didn't you ever ask him anything about it?" I pressed her.

"No, not really," she said, flushing. Then she put her face in her hands and shook her head from side to side mournfully. "Oh, that's not true," she murmured. She was sobbing softly. "Of course I asked him. I told him there had to be something funny about a man hiring him and paying him that way. After I talked to Daddy, he promised me he'd find out more."

She sobbed and couldn't talk for a moment. "I keep thinking, maybe I pushed him into asking questions and that's why . . ."

I sat there quietly. What could I say? Maybe she was right.

Jennifer mopped her eyes and leaned back in the corner of the booth, looking wan and pale and small. "It just gets me crazy! The uncertainty. You don't know who is out there doing this, or why. Dad was down on his luck, you know? He hadn't had a decent part in a long time. There were months at a stretch when he'd be on unemployment. It killed him for me to pay the bills. He'd run elevators, run errands. A forty-eight-year-old man with a college degree running errands. It makes me so damned furious."

I sipped my Schaefer until she ran down. "What do you do?" I asked her.

"I'm an actress," she said, surprised. "Didn't I tell you that? I've got a commercial running now. Have you seen it?"

"What's it about?" I hedged.

"I'm in one of those beer commercials where we're playing volleyball on the beach." She blushed a little. "I know it's kind of dopey, but it pays."

"It all helps."

"And I'm in an off-Broadway play. Do you go to the theater much?"

"Well . . ."

"It's at the Awning on Bleecker Street. *Something That Matters*, it's called. Ever hear of it?"

I had to admit I hadn't.

She laughed a little. "Oh, well, maybe you will now. I play this limousine-liberal society woman who wins the lottery. And I'm up for a *MOW*, but you never know, of course."

"A *MOW*?"

"*Movie of the Week*." She grinned at me, enjoying my ignorance. "I see you're a civilian. I'll have to educate you."

But then, in a moment, her enthusiasm disappeared and she was thinking about her father again. "Poor Papa. The poor, dear man."

"Do you think the guy who was at your apartment is the same one who hired your father?"

Jennifer wagged her head, trying to sort it out. "I don't know. The one at the apartment looked like . . ."

"Like what?"

She looked away. Then she looked back at me. "Like a thug! Like a mobster. He's sort of beefy with dark hair and a big diamond ring."

She studied me, waiting for me to suggest this thug was somebody who might be mixed up in drugs.

"Did you tell Lawler about all this?" I asked, looking for a graceful exit.

"I can't even get him on the phone. That's why I called you."

Yeah, I knew that feeling too. Still, there was nothing for me to write about. An unidentified man came to see her and

15

demanded money he said her father owed him? Maybe it was a legitimate debt.

"But he threatened me, damn it," she said in exasperation. That flintly look was in her eyes again, probably the expression she'd use if she ever played Lady Macbeth.

"How did he threaten you?"

"How?"

"What did he say?"

"He said I'd better give him back the fifty thousand my father took."

"Or what?"

"Or what? What do you think 'or what'?"

"What I think doesn't count."

She gazed at me reflectively with her actress's eyes, and I began to feel myself sliding down into trouble. She was begging for help as she sat there, and I was losing what little noninvolvement I might have had left. That's how reporters get embroiled in stories without really planning to. You talk with people and ask them some questions and the next thing you know you're wrapped inside a puzzle you had no intention of trying to unravel.

"You think you could identify the guy who came to your apartment?" I finally muttered, trying to avoid that look of condemnation.

"Oh, you betcha," she said quickly. "I'll never forget that face. Why?"

"Well, if he was on the boat, they've got a picture of him."

"Who has?"

"Lawler and Santelli."

Well, after that nothing would do but to drag me across town to the Tenth Precinct station house to track down Detective Lawler, the man who didn't return phone calls.

"I've been trying to reach you," Jennifer said accusingly. "Some man came to my apartment and threatened me."

"What?" said Lawler.

"Yes! He said my father had stolen fifty thousand dollars

from him, and he wanted it back. Fitzgerald says you've got a photograph of the man."

It had seemed harmless enough when I'd said it, but now I realized it was a blunder. Big Jim Lawler was not pleased that I'd mentioned those photographs. Cops use surveillance photos to help them solve crimes, but they're not always legal evidence.

"All right," said Lawler. "I was going to ask you to look at those photographs—*alone*. Fitzgerald, I don't want to read about this in the paper. If we've got anybody on this film, I don't want to spook him so he beats it to New Orleans."

"Okay, okay," I said. "But if you do decide to go public with them, I get it first."

Now it was Lawler's turn to mutter, "Okay, okay."

Well, we sat there watching the riverboat unload. Do you have any idea how boring ordinary people doing ordinary things like walking off a boat can be? Fourteen hundred and twelve people strolled down the gangplank lugging picnic baskets, blankets, radios, ice chests, and chairs. Most of them were kids and old people. There was a mixture of younger ones, including the lawyer and his companion, who stood off to one side.

"Who are they?"

"We're working on that," said Lawler. "See anybody you know?"

Jennifer stared and shook her head back and forth as she watched the flickering film of the long line of people straggling by.

"No," she said. "I don't see the man. Or anybody else I know."

Lawler halted the projector and turned on the lights in the squad room.

"Well, there you are," he said.

I realized he was saying there was not much more he could do with the case. I glanced at Jennifer, but she didn't understand the implication at all.

"What should I do about that man?" she said.

"Well, if he comes around again or calls you, let me know."

Jennifer stopped at that. "What? If he walks in on me, how am I going to call you?"

"I'm sorry, Miss Ritter. I don't know what more I can do."

That's the frightful thing about crime. You're on your own most of the time. You can't get a bodyguard unless you're at least a famous Cosa Nostra hit man.

"Thanks," Jennifer Ritter told Lawler. Her voice was forty degrees below zero.

3

Howard Ritter's image receded from my consciousness after that into a long gallery of dimly remembered faces. Like a great, unending river, the people and events you write about in a daily newspaper flow past you day by day, leaving larger or smaller imprints that gradually fade away to nothing. My ancient mentor Marcus Aurelius might have been describing a reporter's outlook when he noted that "man lives only in the present, which is an indivisible point, and all the rest of his life is either past or uncertain." We're not in the business of probing deeply into the cast of characters who slide through our video display terminals or our typewriters. I have written organized crime stories involving a dozen names, and two days later if asked I would be unable to recall one of them. The mind holds the names long enough to write them down, and then they are gone. Nothing is as old as yesterday's news.

I checked with Big Jim Lawler a few times, but there were no breaks. The Howard Ritter murder was pushed slowly backward in Lawler and Santelli's file as new cases landed before them. The bullet that killed Ritter had been fired from a nine millimeter handgun, which meant it could be any one of a large percentage of an estimated one million illegal handguns that exist in New York City.

"What about that lawyer?" I asked.

"Still working on that."

"Anything turn up on Ritter?"

"Clean," said the detective.

So there it was. A minor actor shot to death in the presence of 1,412 people for no apparent reason. Somebody apparently felt Howard Ritter had robbed him and had gone to his daughter's apartment trying to collect, but that person had not gone to the police about it, as far as Lawler could determine. Why? Whoever the man was, he had not been aboard the boat.

"Are you going to bring in each of those people on the film and question them?" Jennifer had wanted to know from Lawler.

"Impossible."

"But why?"

"Miss Ritter, even if I wanted to, I don't have the manpower."

"But one of them has to be a killer!" she raged in frustration.

"Not necessarily."

"What do you mean?"

"Whoever did it might have gotten off the boat without getting his picture taken. We're not absolutely sure we got everybody."

The slug had entered through Ritter's clothes, going through his jacket, sweater, shirt, and undershirt, Lawler explained. There were no powder burns. The angle of the shot suggested it had been fired point-blank, but nothing could be ruled out.

"Not even the possibility that the fatal gunshot was self-inflicted," he said soberly.

"What?" It was a determined, challenging outburst. Jennifer fixed resentful eyes upon this uncaring, hateful policeman. "How can you even consider . . . ?"

"I'm not saying that's what happened," Lawler said, wiping his face and trying to soften it. "I'm only saying we don't know. Until we find the gun, or a motive, or that money . . ."

Jennifer's eyes were boring into Lawler without letup.

"Money?" she said. "Do you actually believe my father took money?"

"We're doing the best we can."

"What are you doing? Please tell me."

Lawler looked at the wall and shook his head. It was a mistake to get on the defensive with the grieving, bitter daughter of a murdered man.

"We've gone over the identities of those on board. We've checked the photographs. We've eliminated most of the boat passengers as probable picnickers. But we still have four hundred people who are possible suspects. We have to hope for a break."

"Such as what?"

"I don't know," he admitted. "Somebody may contact us with a lead."

Jennifer stared ahead blankly, and some of the fury seemed to evaporate. Some of her fight was changing into the helpless resignation people experience when they're up against a frightful tragedy and can do nothing about it.

I didn't see her again after that for a while. Not in person, anyway. But as so often happens when somebody tells you about something you hadn't noticed before, I began spotting her in that television commercial. There she was in a revealing string bikini playing volleyball. She looked so fresh and happy that it hurt to think of that blank stare at the Tenth Precinct. She was lovely, all right, and in trouble, and looking to me for help. I had about as much chance as Frosty the Snowman in Death Valley, but I would never be able to stay out of her life. Still, I wasn't prepared for the way it happened.

I remember it was the night of Bob Samuel's going-away party. He was going to *The New York Times*, like so many others before him. We had a loud bash at Jeanne's in the Hotel Tudor, and I think I had enough Schaefers to fill a tandem truck. I'd become a single since Belinda left for Wales, and I always seemed to be the last one hanging around at a party. So I know it was plenty late when I got home to East Eighty-second Street. I'd sort of halfway fallen into a bloated slumber when the phone rang.

"Yeah?" I mumbled.

"Hey, Fitz." It was Glenn, the night switchboard guy at the *Daily Press*. "Hate to call you at home so late."

"What's up?"

"Well, this broad called and won't stop calling. She said you've got to call her."

I sat up. "Belinda Sharpe?" I said. A shock of fright zigzagged through me at the thought that something dreadful had happened in Wales. "Did the call come from Wales?"

That befuddled Glenn, who handles plenty of nut calls and does not go off the track easily.

"Wales? Naw . . . it's a local call. Jennifer Ritter?"

"Jennifer?"

"She won't stop calling. I told her we can't give out the home phone numbers of reporters. She left her number. You want to call her?"

I scribbled down the number and wondered if I could wait until morning. Some fiend had slipped into the apartment and had put a vise around my head and was gradually squeezing my medulla oblongata into my cerebellum—or maybe vice versa.

I dialed the number painfully, and she answered after about half a ring.

"Hello!"

"Jennifer?"

"Eddie" a terrified voice gasped into the phone.

"What's the matter?"

"Eddie! Oh, my God, is it finally you?"

I tried to concentrate. Her fright spread through me. She was crying and gasping, and I felt that she was just over the line from hysteria.

22

"They came back," she said. "They were here again! I don't know what to do. I'm so afraid."

"Who, Jennifer? The same guy came back?"

"No. A different one."

"Did you call Detective Lawler?"

"He's not on duty. They said call in the morning. I'll be dead by morning."

"Listen, Jenny, I'm on my way. Will you be all right till I get there?"

"Eddie, I can't stay here! I'm helpless, and they keep coming back, and the police won't help me. They came by, but then they left, and I'm alone."

"You want to meet me at Pete's Tavern?"

"Eddie, it's about four o'clock in the morning."

I tried to get my bearings.

"Can I come up there?"

I wish I could tell you I pondered long and hard over her question and that the vision of the lovely Belinda Sharpe hovered in my consciousness. But the only vision flashing through my mind was Jennifer Ritter's vulnerable face, and the only sensation was the fear I had heard rushing through the phone.

"Sure," I said.

I hung up the phone, turned on the light, and looked around. The apartment was in bachelor disarray, with a pile of socks, underwear, and shirts in one corner, several empty Schaefer beer cans scattered around on top of my copies of Marcus Aurelius's *Meditations* and Suetonius's *The Twelve Caesers*, and dishes in the sink as usual.

I cleaned things up a little, but I needn't have bothered. When Jennifer Ritter arrived in a cab and walked in, she wouldn't have cared if the apartment were a thatched hut in the Black Forest with Wotan as her host holding a spear. She walked in in a state of semishock, ready to jump out of her skin. She sat in a kitchen chair and I put a cup of tea in front of her. If it had been a live snake, she wouldn't have noticed.

23

"The guy came back?" I finally asked.

"What?"

"The guy who said he wanted the money—he came back?"

Jennifer shook her head with a mixture of fright and confusion. "No, no, no, Ed. It was a different man!"

"But he wanted the money?"

"Eddie," she said, looking at me in pain and bewilderment, "he was talking about different money."

"What?"

"Yes! He said he wanted the *twenty* thousand dollars Daddy stole."

I looked at her, puzzled.

"Two different people want money they say your father stole?"

Jennifer Ritter nodded blankly. "Maybe I didn't know my father at all," she said.

4

I T'S WONDERFUL TO WAKE up in the morning to smell coffee percolating and hear it softly chug-chugging in the pot. The lovely Belinda Sharpe had slid out of bed so gently that I hadn't noticed, and I didn't come out of it until the aroma floated over me. Then I heard the low murmur of the radio.

"You awake?" she called out, and her voice was strange in my ear. I got up and peeked out, and of course it wasn't Belinda at all, but Jennifer Ritter.

"You awake?" she repeated, looking right at me.

I'm one of those people who can't answer obvious questions such as "You awake?" It's like a person saying "May I ask you something?" You may ask me anything you want, but if you ask me *if* you may ask me, you'll see somebody standing there dumb as a stone.

"I've got to run," she said. "The coffee's ready. I did the dishes. You're some housekeeper."

"Where are you going?" I managed groggily.

"Acting class."

"I thought you were already an actress," I said stupidly.

She laughed. "You never stop studying."

I took a step from the bedroom into the living room, where she'd spent the night on the fold-out couch, and she went skittering across the room to the front door, taking the polar route around the coffee table to avoid coming near me.

"Thanks," she said. "I'll talk to you."

And she was gone.

We were off to a wonderful start.

I stumbled over to the counter in the kitchenette and had some coffee. Already, it was an improvement to have coffee ready when I got up. Belinda had been deliciously efficient that way. I still hadn't gotten over the arrival and departure of Belinda. She had come into my life when her own marriage had broken up and she had launched into a career as a trademark attorney in Manhattan. For several months, we had lived happily like a couple of newlyweds. Then had come urgent news from Wales.

"I've got to go home, Eddie," she had told me.

"What's up?"

"I don't know," she had said. "My uncle has died, and his estate's in a terrible mess. They know I'm a lawyer, and they want me to come home and straighten it out."

There had been nothing I could do. I had no hold on her. Tears and love mingled for a few short, anxiety-filled days until finally she boarded a British Airways 747 and roared into the sky from Kennedy Airport for London and Swansea.

"Bon voyage," I said. "Come back soon."

But the estate trouble had dragged on and on. She had not returned. I no longer knew if she ever would. And now there was Jennifer Ritter.

Jennifer moved in without either of us having figured out what was what. She was pretty eloquent with body language though, her great-circle route around the coffee table telling me in skywriting-sized letters that just because she had moved in, that didn't mean . . .

Didn't mean what?

Even after I'd shaved and climbed into my '69 Ford Falcon to head downtown to the office, I still didn't have a clear idea of what kind of situation I was in. The Falcon sputtered and

26

stalled twice on the way at red lights on Second Avenue. I had picked it up three months before from our Staten Island reporter, Mark Ross, whose father had died and left the old car in his garage. I figured it had to be better than my pumpkin-orange Ford Pinto, which threw off its timing belt every other day for two months and finally slumped into lifelessness in the parking lot at City Hall one afternoon in a plume of blue smoke. Now I wasn't so sure. John, the service-station guy on Second Avenue, told me the Falcon was a real find because it had only twenty-five thousand miles on it. Sometimes I wondered how it had gotten that far.

"It's missing on two cylinders," John said. "Give it a valve job, and it's like new."

I wasn't sure about having a "like new" 1969 Falcon. So I drove it. And stalled. And drove on. Somehow, thinking about my car troubles didn't answer that question about Jennifer's body language.

I sort of halfway asked Jim Owens, the assistant city editor, what he thought. "You ever move in with a girl without really knowing how things stood?" I asked.

"Sure. When I got married," he said.

Lot of help he was.

The first few days after Jennifer moved in were wall-to-wall hectic. Howard Ritter had been cremated in a small private ceremony when the police released his body. Now Jennifer arranged a memorial service at a church on Madison Avenue. Ritter certainly had a lot of friends, all right. Actors, directors, stage-crew people; several hundred turned out and eulogized him as a kind, gentle man. It was a beautiful service, but it put Jennifer on the rack all over again.

It didn't help either when a woman wearing a mink coat and a bloodhound face charged Jennifer and grabbed her in a bear hug.

"Jenny! *Why*?"

"I don't know, Celeste."

Afterward, I drove Jennifer back down to Irving Place so

she could pick up a few more things. She refused to go there alone, and I guess I couldn't blame her. Inside, the gloomy apartment seemed haunted. There were photos on the walls of Howard Ritter in *Man of La Mancha* and in a Coke ad.

Jennifer dug into a desk. "They want his birth certificate," she said with a sardonic chuckle. "Imagine."

She walked over to the telephone and activated the answering machine. "I haven't checked to see if there were any calls for Daddy," she said.

She went back to digging through the desk as we listened to the playback of the tape. There were several calls from an agent, obviously made before Howard's death.

Then a strange voice came on. "Howie?" it said, and it wasn't an ordinary voice. "Listen, Mr. Goodman wants you again. Here's the number. Five-two-eight, seven-nine-four-two. Call me back, Schweethaht."

Jennifer was standing frozen at the desk, listening.

"Play it again!"

I wound the tape and played it again. This time it was clear who was talking. Humphrey Bogart!

"Who's that?" I asked her.

She shrugged. "It must be the man who hired Daddy! He's disguising his voice."

We played the tape several more times, but the voice was always tauntingly distant, hiding behind Humphrey Bogart. Was it Mr. Goodman? Or somebody who worked for him?

"Try the number," said Jennifer.

I dialed the number that had been left on the recording device. No answer. I tried it again. And again. Then I called Moony Rand at the telephone company. He had once worked at the *Daily Press*. He said he could locate the phone for me as long as it wasn't an unlisted number. In a few moments he had it.

"Pay phone in Times Square, Fitz."

Jennifer suddenly began pacing around, an idea brewing. "Wait a minute," she said. "Wait a minute! Daddy used to pick up the payments from Goodman at Actors Equity! He'd get half in advance and half afterward. It was left for him in an envelope."

"He never met this Goodman?"

"Not that he told me. Only the chauffeur or some man . . . I don't know."

"Where is Actors Equity?" Now I was pacing too.

"Just off Times Square," said Jennifer, halting and looking at me. "On West Forty-sixth Street."

"Did your father know people there?"

Jennifer gave me one of those looks a person casts at you when you ask if it would be dangerous to climb into a cage with an enraged gorilla at the Bronx Zoo.

"Well, of course—he knew everybody there," she said.

"Did he go there much?"

"Eddie, he went there every day. Religiously. We all have to go check the board to see if there are any jobs."

We looked at each other, both thinking the same thing. She said it first. "The guy's got to be an actor! He hangs around Equity. He knows Daddy. Actors are always impersonating people's voices. He probably called Daddy from a pay phone right outside."

I had to think she was right. This Humphrey Bogart who worked for Goodman—he knew Howard Ritter.

Jennifer put in a phone call to Equity, but it was too late. They were closed. She gathered up her father's papers, which included an insurance policy from Columbia National Insurance Company, and we drove to East Eighty-second Street.

Until that night, Jennifer had been sleeping in the living room on the fold-out sofa, if you could call her restless turnings sleep. Several times, I had almost gone to her. But on this night, our situation had clearly undergone an evolution.

"It was really sweet of you to take me in," she said, moving over to sit beside me on the sofa. She curled her legs under her and stared at me quizzically.

"You're a funny guy, you know that?" She reached out to

touch me, anxious to clarify. "I don't mean *funny* . . . I mean nice."

I wouldn't be surprised if I blushed at that.

She let out a little, happy laugh. "But, wow, you sure do cover it up!"

"What do you mean?" I protested.

"You *do*! Everything's inside. If I hadn't gotten to know you a little, I'd think you were . . . I don't know . . . indifferent. But you're really just shy, aren't you?"

I said something brilliant like, "I don't know."

"Come on . . . tough reporter! It's just a sham. You're a genuinely nice guy. You read everything, you care . . . but when I first met you I thought you were a steamroller. How many people really know you?"

"How many people really know anybody?"

She was sitting very close now, and I was tumbling into those bottomless brown eyes. I swam in the lovely sensation of her mouth on mine and her arms holding me close.

Not even the Apollo Belvedere could have resisted such a delicious and tempting invitation. The nearness and the dizzying female perfume of Jenny engulfed me, overwhelmed me, lifted me into an orbit beyond the far side of the moon. We glided through galaxies that no one has ever succeeded in adequately describing.

Over and over again, I promised Jennifer of the bottomless eyes and lithe, silken embrace that I would track down every possible lead; that I would explore the misty moons of Saturn to help her. Under the circumstances, how could I promise less?

5

I WAS ON GENERAL assignment on the 11:00 A.M. to 7:00 P.M. shift, and Ironhead had gotten it into his head to make a feature writer out of me.

One day Jim Owens had tossed me the weather story, and what the hell are you going to write about when it's just an ordinary freezing day? Well, I had this bright idea and called up the Bronx Zoo and "interviewed" a polar bear. I had the polar bear complain about the lousy heat wave, see, and long for a decent blizzard and some nice, tasty icicles.

Ironhead went nuts over the story. He's already nuts, if you ask me, but that's something else. If you want to know, I think maybe the publisher's wife, Mrs. McFadden, liked it, and so that's why Ironhead got all worked up. Once Tom Reilly "interviewed" a statue in Central Park, and Mrs. McFadden virtually lost her equilibrium over that idea. For about a year after that, every time anything happened, poor Tom Reilly was dispatched to Central Park or the Metropolitan Museum to interview a new statue to see what it thought about Nancy Reagan's new knickers, or whether the Islanders would win another Stanley Cup.

That's the way it is with editors. Once you write something that catches their fancy, they keep giving you the same kind of story and they get it into their head that that's the only thing you can do. It keeps up until you get stuck with a tugboat strike, and then you're the tugboat-strike writer for the next million years.

"You've developed a nice, light touch, Fitz," said Ironhead, beslobbering his cigar in his truly disgusting way. "See if you can do something with this."

I was to go to the New York Coliseum and interview a female psychologist from Seton Hall University in New Jersey who had written a thesis to the effect that men drive cars as though they're knights in armor in the days of King Arthur.

"See, this broad says you guys get in your Jaguars, and you think you're Sir Lancelot with a goddamn lance sticking out from under the hood, because you're full of aggression and bullshit."

Tom Reilly happened to overhear Ironhead and, being a typical smart-ass, started guffawing. "You think Fitz drives a *Jaguar*?" he chortled. "If that rolling ashcan were an animal, it'd be something revolting like a goddamn anteater."

Reilly is a big, round bear with a handlebar mustache. He wears a New York Yankees baseball cap in the city room when he isn't wearing a derby. He reminds me of Frankie Wagner, who came to the paper from one of those leftish radical weeklies that flourished for a while in the Big Apple. Frankie was hired by somebody upstairs and thrust upon Ironhead. He carried on what I used to call bomb-toss reporting—he was convinced that all public officials were contemptible frauds— which, of course, was true in a lot of cases. Anyway, after a few weeks Frankie stopped wearing his Edwardian blue blazer and started dressing like "the people" he was out there fighting for. Ragged jeans. A blue work shirt. Yellow work shoes. Then he got this punched-in hat that was tied on with a string, and grew a full beard like Walt Whitman. He was assigned to cover the Sanitation Department and everybody called him the Duke of Debris.

Ironhead noticed this goddamn Trader Horn Okie outfit one day and stood there looking Frankie up and down, speechless. "Frankie," he finally said, "I think we've gone about as far as we can with you." Frankie left, denouncing the *Press* as another sellout journalistic compost heap.

But it was about then that the suit and the sport jacket and the dress started vanishing from the city room. People started wearing whatever the hell they pleased, from Irish sweaters to jeans and cowboy boots. Don Harrington took up T-shirts that said things like HACKENSACK WATER COMPANY or something. So when Reilly showed up, right out of Yale, he claimed, he fit right in.

I had promised to meet Jennifer at Actors Equity sometime in the afternoon if I could get out of the office. Ironhead's assignment worked out just right. I got out at about five o'clock, and was supposed to head over to the Auto Show at Columbus Circle. I drove the Falcon to the West Side, parked in an NYP zone on West Forty-fourth Street, and walked up from Times Square, past the statue of George M. Cohan, to Equity. On the second floor, there was a hallway sitting area and an information desk and then the large actors' lounge overlooking the street.

I don't know what I expected, but Equity was a beehive of actors milling about. There they stood or sat, all busily reading *Variety*, *Backstage*, and *Show Business*, and checking the notices on the bulletin boards. There must have been a couple of hundred actors and actresses in the two rooms. How to pick Humphrey Bogart out of the swirling scene?

Jennifer spotted me and hurried over. "Hi," she said a little breathlessly. She had that wonderful, lithe actress look that melted me. She glanced quickly around the lounge, scanning the faces, while I was scanning her. She caught me at it, and smiled.

"How do we start?" I asked her.

"I know! The information desk! You can leave messages."

She hurried to the desk outside the lounge, where a diminutive gray-haired lady sat at a desk.

"Hi, Miss Grady." She smiled, and the woman beamed.

"Jenny!" she cried, and jumped up to come over to the counter. "I saw your commercial! It was so cute! I haven't seen you for a while . . ."

Miss Grady's words suddenly stopped. She blinked, and looked down, and then back up, her face red with embarrassment. "Oh, I haven't seen you since before . . . I read it in the paper."

"I know," Jennifer soothed her. "I know."

"He was such a dear man," Miss Grady murmured sadly.

"Yes, he was. I was just wondering, do you know if anyone left any messages for Daddy here recently?"

"Oh, yes," she chirped, eager to help. "Yes . . . but he got them. There was an envelope. A couple of them, I remember. And a plastic thing."

"What kind of a plastic thing?" I asked.

"It was red, like something you take to the beach."

"Beach?"

"That's what it looked like to me," she said, trying to remember. "I thought it was one of those little inflatable things you float on in a swimming pool." Miss Grady blushed a little. "It was in a large envelope, and I looked inside to see what it was because I didn't know where it had come from. I just took a peek. It was folded flat, you know."

"Do you remember who left any of the things?" asked Jennifer.

The woman went blank and shook her head. "No, I don't. You know, I don't think I ever even talked to the person. They were left on the counter here, with Mr. Ritter's name on them."

She shook her head slowly. "You know, I wondered about that after . . . after I saw it in the paper. I don't know who left them."

"Do you remember how many envelopes were left?" I asked her.

"Two or three," she said. "I think three."

"What were they like?"

"Like?"

"Any kind of return address or printing on them?"

"Just Actors Equity envelopes," she said. "There's a stack of them on the table over there. I'm so sorry, Jenny."

We drifted away, and Jennifer was suddenly walking rigidly. We were in the same room where the killer must have been. He or she could be there even now. We glanced around, suddenly searching every face for signs of intrigue. It was absurd.

We sat on a large sofa in the lounge on the Forty-sixth Street side and Jennifer lighted a cigarette with trembling hands. She blew out smoke and stared straight ahead.

"I knew it," she murmured. "He's an actor! He must be in and out of here all the time. All we have to do is wait."

I looked at her. "Wait for what?"

"Humphrey Bogart!"

I shook my head, trying to clear it, as though that would also clear Jennifer's. "Jenny, how are you going to know him?"

"Sooner or later, he'll do his Humphrey Bogart thing," she said.

"I don't think that's going to work," I said envisioning the two of us sitting there for ten years eavesdropping on conversations.

"Got any better ideas?" she said, looking at me.

"I guess not," I admitted.

She puffed on her cigarette and darted glances around. "We can wait and see."

An unhappy spasm went through me, and I involuntarily glanced at my watch. "I don't think I can stay."

"Why not?"

"I'm on a story."

"What story?"

"The Auto Show."

The words came out of my mouth like lead and thumped onto the floor. What an insultingly trivial assignment when she was trying to find out who killed her father. The Auto

Show! It hung in the air, ready to be skewered, dried, tanned, stuffed, and mounted, and labeled for what it was: worthless pap.

"Well, okay." She smiled uncomplainingly. "I think I'll stick around for a while anyway."

I think it was at that moment it first became evident to me that this was the beginning of an extremely touchy situation involving a potentially explosive triangle.

In one corner of the triangle was the brave and lovely Jennifer, who desperately needed my help. At another corner was a smoldering, unexploded bomb known as Ironhead Matthews, my city editor, who held unswervingly and deafeningly to the opinion that he and no one else decided what stories his reporters would pursue.

The third corner, of course, was an insignificant ink-stained wretch who was certain to be tugged and yanked in every direction until he didn't know his hypotenuse from the other sides: to wit, me. Possibly I should have realized this sooner, but I was never any good at geometry.

The reason the triangle was potentially explosive was that Ironhead did not think my assignment was to work on the Howard Ritter murder, and yet if I deserted the appealing actress in her travail, I felt I deserved to be shipped immediately to the Attica Correctional Facility.

"Well, maybe I can stick around for a while," I mumbled. It seemed like an innocent enough remark at the time.

We sat on a sofa by the window and watched, Jennifer smoking a cigarette and I chewing nervously on a Tiparillo. After a while, most of the actors drifted out, and there was only a gray-haired man and an elderly woman sitting together talking about residuals. The man looked like Edmund Muskie and the woman like Nancy Walker. Neither looked much like Bogart.

Jennifer was slumped back against the couch.

"Why don't we go have a drink?" I suggested.

6

JENNIFER LOOKED GLUM AS we walked out of Equity and down Seventh Avenue through Times Square.

"There's a place Daddy used to go," she said as we reached Forty-fifth Street. She led me down Forty-fifth toward Eighth Avenue to a little place called the Theatre Bar. We walked inside and sat at the bar just inside the door. The place was fairly shabby and fairly empty, the sort of place actors could afford.

A swarthy, husky bartender with heavy eyebrows walked down to us. "What'll it be?" he asked pleasantly in a gravelly voice.

"Are you Angie?" Jennifer asked him, and the bartender's face lighted up.

"Yeah! Angie Pinzino."

"My father used to come in here," she said. "Maybe you knew him. Howard Ritter. He was an actor."

"Sure," Angie smiled. "Howard the actor." Then the smile slid off his face and he nodded sympathetically. "Oh, yeah, I heard about that." He looked away. "Too bad."

We ordered drinks and Angie served us, chatting away aimlessly to cover the awkwardness of the situation. When he put the drinks in front of us, he finally ran down. "Well, what can you say, huh?"

"Is there a Mr. Goodman who comes in here?" I asked.

Angie pondered that. "Goodman . . . Goodman . . . doesn't ring a bell."

"He hired my father to make deliveries," said Jennifer.

Angie shook his head. He couldn't help on that one.

"The person that called," I tried again, "disguised his voice like Humphrey Bogart. Anybody who comes in here do Bogart?"

Angie laughed at that. "Well . . . hell . . . listen, we get lots of actors in here, you know? Especially on unemployment-check day."

"You wouldn't happen to know somebody who does Humphrey Bogart imitations?" I asked.

"Oh, there's got to be some," he laughed. "There's a bunch of comics that hang around here."

"Any of them here now?" I asked, looking down the bar. The place was starting to fill up with the after-work crowd.

Angie glanced around. "Naw, don't see them. You can catch them late, though, after the clubs close."

"The comics work the clubs around here?"

Angie smiled. "Oh, sure. You want to hear Bogart, go to the clubs."

"Which ones?" Jennifer piped up.

"Oh, lots of them," said Angie. "The Improv, over on Forty-fourth, Catch a Rising Star, Going Up, lots of them."

Angie walked away down the bar, and suddenly Jennifer was all excited. "Sure," she said, tugging at my arm, "those clubs . . . that's where they try out their material."

I lighted a Tiparillo and tried to think.

Jennifer was in full sail. "It figures," she rushed on. "Daddy must have known these guys. The guy has to be a comic! One of them is Bogart. All we have to do is find him."

We sat in the Theatre Bar and I had a couple more beers. Jennifer begged off, though, because she had to be at the Awning Theatre downtown for her show. Angie had told us that the Improv and the other comedy clubs started at about nine every night and went on into the early hours of the morning.

"We can go by after the play," Jennifer told me, leaning forward and holding my hands on the table. "We'll find Humphrey Bogart at one of them, I'm sure of it."

It was nice to see hope flashing in her eyes.

"Say," she remarked, "you *still* haven't seen my play!"

I groaned. She was right, of course.

"Why don't you come down and see it. Then afterward we can go to the Improv?"

Putty. Shapeless, spineless, brainless putty. I wish I could tell you that I didn't drive her down to Bleecker Street to the Awning and see the play. Not that she wasn't good, or that the play wasn't a lot of fun. She was, and it was. Jennifer was this Gloria-Steinem-emerging-to-self-discovery-type society woman who wins $100,000 in the lottery and gives it to the only poor person she knows—her black maid. Her maid's son turns out to be a Black Panther. Don't ask me to explain the plot, because any play sounds goofy if you do.

Anyway, afterward I went backstage to meet Jenny in her rat cage of a dressing room under the stage, which was about three feet square.

"Did you like it?" she bubbled, jumping up to hold my hands and search my face eagerly.

I had to laugh. "Sure I liked it. And you were something . . . I just can't get over it. You were terrific."

And then she was in my arms, hugging and beaming. "Just let me change."

The Improv is a small night club on West Forty-fourth Street, where hopeful stand-up comics get up on a little stage and try out their routines in front of cynical, surly, and often tipsy audiences. The club, and the others like it, pays the poor devils nothing, but the devils keep coming because once in a great while one of them actually gets a job on television or in the Catskills.

Jerry Stiller and Anne Meara had once been on the little Improv stage, and so had Steve Landesberg, who later was a regular on *Barney Miller*. Inside we were shown to a postage-stamp sized table near the small platform stage, and a stream of comics paraded before us.

It was obvious right away why most of them didn't get paid, and never would get paid anywhere. One guy's routine was almost entirely toilet humor. Then there was the guy who did Polish and black jokes. There was the angry Queens girl who did the feminist and Jewish jokes. It was self-destructive humor. Some of them were funny in desperate, hysterical ways, and there were plenty of imitations of Ronald Reagan and Nixon and Mayor Koch and cabdrivers.

One guy called himself Trigger Moran, and he was the Irish-joke-Catholic-school-humor guy. After a couple of vile gags about nuns, a girl in the audience yelled something.

Trigger Moran apparently was used to fielding verbal missles from the tables because he didn't miss a beat. He glanced in the general direction of the voice, drew himself up, and lisped: "Of all the gin joints in all the towns in all the world, she walks into mine."

The place broke up, and there was sudden pain in my ankle where Jennifer kicked me.

"It's him!" she hissed in my ear.

7

I WATCHED TRIGGER MORAN on the little stage. He was slim and insignificant, and had an arrogant weasel face. He wore shapeless brown cords and a T-shirt with ATLANTIC CITY written across it in gold script. Before I could figure out what to do, Jennifer got up and worked her way back through the crowded aisle out of the room.

Trigger Moran apparently got his name for his quick comebacks, because after his first Humphrey Bogart ad lib, he was assailed from all sides by kids telling him that he was a creep, a pimp, a dork, a jerk, a kielbasa, and a variety of things scatological.

"Thanks, Schweethaht," he drawled.

Then Jenny slid back in beside me."

"Damn!" she muttered. "I can't reach him!"

"Who?"

"Lawler! The man's never there!"

"For chrissake, it's eleven o'clock," I told her. "Lawler works the day tour."

"But none of the other detectives wants to hear about somebody else's case," she said in frustration. " 'Call tomorrow.' I could be dead tomorrow!"

What could you say? Detectives don't often jump into

another officer's case on another tour unless it's so hot it can't be ignored.

"What the hell were you going to do—have him arrested?"

"Yes," she hissed. "Shouldn't we?"

"Maybe we ought to talk to him first," I suggested.

I sat there trying to think of a way to entice Trigger Moran and his weasel face over to the table. I could buy him a drink, of course.

"He probably needs a job," I told Jennifer. "Maybe we could pretend to interview him for some club."

"That's it," Jennifer snapped. "We're looking for somebody who can do Humphrey Bogart!"

"If he's really in on it, he won't talk to Ritter's daughter," I said. "Or to a reporter, either."

"Let me do the talking," she said.

Well, the capture of the little murderer of Jennifer's father couldn't be easier, it seemed. Because just then he leaned out over the stage and glared quizzically at us. "If you two want to plan your orgy," he flung at us, "I can always go take a leak."

He got a cheap laugh with that, but it opened the door for us. When he hopped down off the stage to a smattering of applause, Jennifer waved him over.

"Hi," she gushed. "I'm sorry we were talking. We were just so impressed with you."

Trigger Moran smiled and sat down. "Yeah?"

"My friend and I are going to produce a revue," she said, "and we're looking for new talent." This revelation certainly surprised me, but not half as much as the ones that followed.

"I'm Jennifer Crawford," she smiled. "And this is Dave Kingman." I realized she meant me.

"Not the ballplayer," she added. "The other one." The other Dave Kingman smiled hopefully.

"We're looking for someone who can do Humphrey Bogart," said Jennifer. "Somebody told me you're the best around."

A mugger could not have gotten Trigger Moran's attention more completely. He sat there more or less hypnotized, listening to this good fortune descending upon him. Jennifer certainly understood actors. Finally he found his tongue.

"Well, say, listen—sure, I can do Bogart! A revue? You mean off-Broadway or off-off?"

"Oh, Broadway," smiled Jennifer. "David insists on that." I smiled insistingly.

"When are you opening?" Trigger wanted to know.

"We're not sure yet," said Jennifer. "But I just want to know how to reach you. Will you be working here tomorrow night?"

"Sure, probably," he said eagerly. "Let me give you my home number and my service."

Jennifer glanced at me, pleased with her successful gambit, as Trigger wrote out his numbers. Then I heard it, and so did Jennifer.

"Here's looking at you, kid." It floated lispingly out over us. We looked at the stage. There was another Humphrey Bogart in an orange sweater doing his thing.

"Who's that?" Jennifer asked Trigger Moran.

Moran glanced up sourly. "That's Jason Murdoch. You don't want him. He's no good."

We certainly didn't want another Bogart, since it cast doubt on the first one. And unfortunately, that wasn't the end of it. We hit several other of these comic clubs that night, too, and found at least one Bogart in each one of them.

We also soon realized that a lot of the same comics showed up at all the clubs. They would do a bit at one club and then rush to the next one and wait their turn.

Finally we ended up at a place called Going Up, on West Forty-ninth Street. It was in the basement, with a bar in the front and a little stage and tables in the back, and the smell of pot smoke in the air. More or less keeping charge was an emcee named Barney Wells with blown-back blond hair and a gold chain around his neck.

"New York, ya gotta love it," Barney cooed in a fine, shellacked voice. "There's a busted head for every light on Broadway."

A shrill, self-conscious laugh exploded in our ears. It came from the waitress, who was standing by our little table.

"Isn't he something?" she confided to us. "Funniest man in New York." She was moon-faced, with dark, wide eyes and black curls piled on top of her head like Napoleon's Josephine. "What can I bring you?"

Barney Wells was sailing again. "And here's one of those busted heads now . . ."

It was that, all right. Orange-sweater Jason Murdoch again, whom we had already heard twice that night.

We walked out of Going Up and drove back over to the Theatre Bar for a last drink with Angie and a post mortem on our scheme. Jenny was downcast. I couldn't think of much to say either.

"Any luck?" Angie asked us.

"Yeah," I murmured. "Too much. Everybody does Bogart."

"Yeah," Angie nodded.

Then some of the comics drifted in, as Angie had said they would, and when they spotted us they all started elbowing each other. I heard a muffled "producers" floating over. Barney Wells, the emcee from Going Up, stared at us the hardest of all, apparently annoyed that nobody had told him about us earlier and he hadn't had a chance to throw *his* Bogart at us. Thank God for small favors.

We drove glumly back down to Gramercy Park, and I parked the green bomb near Jenny's apartment. Jennifer wanted to get the Humphrey Bogart tape so we could listen to it more carefully, maybe sort out the right voice, and get Detective Jim Lawler interested.

We rode up in the elevator, and as the elevator door opened we heard a car backfire in the street. It came across loud and sharp, like a firecracker, and suddenly I realized it wasn't from the street and it wasn't a backfire. It was a gunshot. I must have tensed, because Jennifer suddenly looked at me.

"What's the matter?"

"Shhhh!"

"What?"

I edged off the elevator and looked down the corridor toward the Ritter apartment. There was a shadow where the door ought to have been.

"Your door's open," I told her softly.

"Oh, my God," she said.

I stepped out into the corridor to get a better look. The door was open, all right, and there was a dog or a kid in the doorway. Then the kid or dog stood up and turned into a man. He had been bending over something in the doorway.

Not only a man, but a man glaring at us down the hall with a gun in his hand.

He raised the gun and pointed it at me. I shoved myself and Jennifer violently back into the elevator as a shot crashed through the corridor.

BANG!

I banged my fist against every button on the control panel of the elevator as we heard heavy steps thumping along the hall toward us. The elevator doors began moving in agonizingly slow motion. A million years later the door finally closed. Frantic pounding on the door. A husky, guttural, Neanderthal shouting.

The indifferent elevator swayed leisurely upward, immune to our shouts to go faster. I felt a frigid chill spreading through me, which was easy to recognize as terror.

"Who was it?" Jennifer managed.

"A guy with a gun!"

"Did you recognize him?"

"All I saw was the gun! Shut up!"

She looked at me in surprise, but I had no time for civilities. What to do? Would he race up the stairs and be waiting for us at the top? Would he beat it downstairs and get the hell away from here?

"How many floors in this building?" I snapped.

"Uh . . . twelve . . ."

"Do you know anybody on nine, ten, or eleven?"

"Uh . . . let me think . . ."

"Don't think . . . tell me!"

"Ten!"

I punched the tenth floor button again savagely. "What apartment?"

"Oh, God! I don't know! To the right . . . third door."

The elevator shuddered to a halt on ten. I stuck my head out and looked both ways. Nothing. "Come on!" I dragged her down the hall to the third door on the right and began pounding on it.

"Who lives here?" I asked Jennifer. "Call her name."

"Katie!" Jennifer yelled, banging on the door. "Katie! It's me . . . Jenny Ritter!"

". . . hello . . . who's there?" A trembly, high voice like a frightened rodent.

"Katie, it's Jenny Ritter! Open the door!"

"What's the matter? It's four o'clock!"

I shoved Jennifer out of the way, and adopted a hopefully commanding tone of voice. "Open up there! Police!"

The rodent squealed and chains clunked. The door opened. There stood a tiny woman with her hair in curlers wearing a blue terry-cloth robe and glasses like the bottoms of Coke bottles.

"What's the matter?"

I shoved Jennifer in ahead of me and closed the door behind us. "Where's the phone?" I demanded. Katie pointed mutely to a phone on a table. I jumped to it, snatched it up, and dialed the precinct number.

"What's the matter, Jenny?"

"I'm sorry to barge in on you like this, Katie, but . . . there's a man . . ."

"What?"

"A man with a gun is chasing us!"

I thought the rodent would jump up to the chandelier. She hopped backward skittishly, her mouth open and working. Nothing came out.

"Thirteenth Precinct. Officer Duddy," said this laconic voice.

I blurted out our tale of woe, which caused Katie to hop backwards some more.

I heard a car starting up, and jumped to the window of Katie's apartment to look out. On the street, a large, black car had its lights on. The car crashed backward into a parked car behind it, then lurched out into East Nineteenth Street. I was too high up and it was too dark to see much. The car gunned its engine and raced down the block.

"I'm going to have a look," I said. "Don't open the door till the police get here."

Katie was hopping around like a duck on a hot stove by now. "I shouldn't have opened the door!" she shrieked. "The neighborhood's gone!"

"You'll be all right," I said.

And Katie ran into the bathroom and locked the door.

"I'm coming with you," said Jennifer, moving behind me toward the door.

"I think that was him driving away. At least I hope it was."

We went back along the corridor and inched down the stairs to Jenny's floor. I peeked down the hall. The shadow was still there. The door to her apartment was still standing open. We walked cautiously along the hall to her door until we were close enough to make out what the man with the gun had been bending over.

There were two feet just inside the door, and the body of a man was sprawled on the floor face down with his head pointing into the apartment. He was as still as a wooden plank.

Jenny gasped, hid her face, and began crying in terrified little chirps.

"Where's the light?"

"Just inside the door . . . right side."

I stepped in cautiously over the sprawled form on the floor and switched on the light. The apartment was empty except for the body. I leaned down to look at the man, and saw a stain spreading outward on the rug from his chest.

8

EVERYBODY KNOWS THAT finding a cop when you need one is a problem, but call 911 and say you've discovered a body on the living-room floor with a stain spreading from his chest, and you've got cop cars lighting up the street with revolving red lights and detectives and even a detective sergeant swarming all over you. Fresh blood is about the only thing that will get you a cop in a hurry.

It was about four in the morning, which was past the last deadline of the *Daily Press*, but I called Rick Mazzilli at the city desk and told him what I knew.

"You don't know who he is?" Rick wanted to know.

"Not yet. The cops are on the way."

"Let me know if he's anybody important. We could replate if it's a councilman. If you're gonna find bodies, Fitz, make it at a decent hour, huh?"

I hung up. Another guy shot to death in Manhattan is about as unusual as a camel race in Saudi Arabia.

The thing about finding a body is that the cops want you to explain its presence. Even if you don't live there.

"What's this?" is the way a short, barrel-chested detective in a tan suit put it when he walked in. He was looking at me.

"You got me."

"Who is he?"

"We just walked in and there he was."

The tan suit introduced himself as Detective Third Grade Russell Tate, and said he was catching at the Thirteenth Precinct Squad, which means he was the only one on duty when the call came in.

Tate looked at Jennifer Ritter, who sat on the sofa on the other side of the room in a state of shock. "You know who this is?" Detectives seemed to be forever asking her to identify dead bodies.

Jennifer could only shake her head from side to side.

"Did you look?"

Jennifer shook her head again.

Tate squatted on the carpet, looking at the body. Its feet were toward the door, its head pointing into the room.

"Looks like he opened the door and stepped in, and somebody let him have it," said Tate. He got up, lit a cigarette and glanced at Jennifer and then at me.

"Did you hear anything? See anything?"

I told him about finding Jennifer's apartment door open and about the man who took a shot at me.

"Did you get a look at him?" he wanted to know.

"I saw his gun, that's about all," I said. "He drove a big black car. At least, I think that was him."

"What if we'd come in earlier?" Jennifer shuddered. "Whoever it was would have shot one of us! Maybe he's after me!"

"Now, take it easy," said the soft-voiced plainclothesman.

"Sure, take it easy," sneered Jennifer. "Your apartment isn't a shooting gallery! I told Lawler they'd be back!"

"You told who?" asked Bruce.

I explained about Howard Ritter and that Detective Lawler of the Tenth Precinct had the case. Detective Tate nodded his head and told one of the uniform cops to phone Lawler at home. I winced.

Well, an assistant medical examiner and a police photographer and a lab crew all looked over the dead man on the floor, and drew a chalk line around his figure on the rug. It seemed to take forever. They were about through when in walked a tall, thoroughly annoyed, half-awake apparition with a sour expression on his face.

"Sorry, Jim," the tan-suit detective said, making a sympathetic face. "Hated to wake you, but it's your case."

"Yeah, yeah," Lawler mumbled, yawning, and then lit a cigarette. He turned his sleepy eyes on us.

"Now what have you done?" he demanded. He walked over and squatted down by the body. "Can we turn him over?" he asked.

They turned him over so we could see his face. Jennifer looked and gasped, "Oh, my God! It's him!"

"Who?"

"That man who came here looking for money!"

The dead man was well tanned, with styled hair, and wore a fashionable blue blazer with a designer label. He certainly didn't appear to be an ordinary house burglar. Lawler went through his pockets and found a wallet stuffed with cash and credit cards. Then he saw his side jacket pocket was bunched and stretched toward the floor. He reached in and pulled out a handgun.

"Well, well," he said, taking the revolver by the trigger guard and holding it up. "He came here with iron."

I thought Jennifer might faint at the sight of the revolver, but instead she came over closer, looking furious.

"What? He came here with a gun? I told you it wasn't safe here! But no—you don't care! Now do you believe me, for God's sake? They both had guns!"

Lawler gathered up the man's papers and cards and walked over to a coffee table, where he laid them all out neatly like he was dealing a hand of solitaire.

"Who is he?" I said, sitting beside him on the sofa. Jennifer came over and sat on the other side of Lawler.

"Looks like somebody named Harry Berg," said Lawler.

51

"Harry Berg?" I looked quizzically at Jennifer. She shook her head slowly. "He's a small time thug on the fringes of the mob," Lawler said.

Jennifer reached toward me with a trembling white hand. "Give me one of those, will you?" she asked, pointing at my Tiparillo. I unwrapped one of the slim little cigars and gave it to her. She picked up a book of matches from the coffee table and lighted the cigar. Her hand and the Tiparillo shook like a branch in a strong breeze.

"Can you grasp it?" she said in a tremulous voice. "People you don't even know coming after you with guns?" She walked across the room to the fireplace and stood there hugging herself with both arms as though warding off a chill.

Lawler carefully gathered up the ID papers, picking up the plastic ones by the edges in case there were fingerprints. He strolled after her, thinking police-officer thoughts.

"You say this man was here before?"

"I told you!"

"He wanted money your father had taken from him?"

"That's what he said."

"How much did he say was involved?"

"Uh . . . fifty thousand," said Jennifer. "But it's ridiculous. My father didn't have money like that."

"Ummm," said Lawler, making little jottings in his notebook. He was clicking away like a computer whose insides are digesting statistics. "And another guy was here wanting . . ."

"Twenty thousand."

"Do you have any idea what connection your father might have had with the expired subject or the other one who came here?"

"No, no, no," Jennifer burst out, becoming impatient and snappish. "But it has to be about that Mr. Goodman!"

"The one who hired him to make deliveries?"

"Yes. What else could it be?"

"Did you see him again after the first time he was here?" Lawler tried again.

"No."

"Did you know his identity before now?"

"What? No. Why are you asking me these things?" Jennifer snapped.

"Ordinary procedure in homicides," he growled. "How long have you been here?"

"I don't know. Maybe an hour."

"Yes. We were just coming out of the elevator when we heard the first shot."

Lawler picked up on that. "There was more than one shot?"

"The second one was at me," I told him.

"I gather he missed?"

"Yes."

"Hmmm."

That didn't seem to interest him much.

Lawler looked from one of us to the other for a few minutes and then went over and whispered to the assistant medical examiner. The A.M.E. cocked his head and scratched his neck and then he whispered back. Lawler strolled back over to us.

"What time was it when you got to the door?"

"I don't know," I said. "After three."

"Three-thirty?"

"Close to that. Why?"

Lawler was walking around in little circles now, gazing at Jennifer and then at me. "Did you make a phone call to the precinct earlier?" he asked Jennifer.

"Yes," she said. "Why aren't you ever there?"

"Listen, I work eight to four, see? Then I have a second job, see? Just answer the questions. Where did you call from?"

"Where?"

"Did you make the call from this apartment?"

"No," said Jennifer. "From a nightclub."

The words came out sotto voce, a sarcastic comment on our different life-styles: "Nightclub." He sighed and looked at us again. "Why did you call from there?"

"We were looking for Humphrey Bogart."

Lawler closed his eyes in pain. "Please."

Jennifer explained. "We thought the man who had called and disguised his voice was the one who shot Daddy." She glanced at the dead body. "I guess we were wrong."

Lawler had his notebook out again and was making little jottings. "Miss Ritter, do you own a firearm?"

"No," said Jenny, and then she realized what he had said. "No!"

Lawler looked at me. "Fitzgerald?"

"Are you suspecting *us*?" Jennifer blurted. "Are you trying to say we were here when he was shot? We were at the Improv when I called!"

"Can someone verify that?"

Jennifer's eyes widened. "He *does* suspect us!"

"It's my job to check out everything," Lawler said rather lamely.

"Yes," Jennifer snapped. "Somebody can verify it. About a hundred people! That comic . . . Trigger Moran . . . he can tell you. And several others."

"Hmmmm," said Lawler. He walked around some more. "I think it would be advisable for you not to stay here for a while."

"Don't worry about that. The Gestapo couldn't keep me here."

"What do you think?" I asked Lawler.

The lanky cop wagged his head and rubbed his face. "Howard Ritter was mixed up in something, that's for sure."

Jennifer sank onto the sofa and a cry of anguish came out. "Don't say that."

"Why else would they try to shake him down?"

"Why?" Jennifer's eyes had shrunk and by now they were tiny, glowing glass beads. "I don't know. But nothing will get done if the police won't even pay attention! I can never find you!"

Lawler exploded. "Listen, you," he yelled. "I don't appreciate you dragging me out of bed in the middle of the night."

54

"I didn't drag you," snapped Jennifer, pointing at the dead body. "He did."

The next thing I knew he had turned on me. "Listen, Fitzgerald, you'd better tell your friend here we're only trying to help!"

"Huh?" I'm afraid I said. If they thought I was in control of the Planet Ritter, they had another thought coming. There I was, caught between an angry, dead-on-his-feet cop and a terrified woman who was frantic with fear. It was the worst triangle yet.

I sat beside Jennifer and took her hand. I hated to admit it, but I found myself agreeing with Big Jim Lawler that Howard Ritter had been mixed up in something. That shot down the corridor at us was a convincing argument. And now Howard Ritter wasn't the only one mixed up in it. The guy had seen me.

9

I DON'T KNOW WHEN we got to East Eighty-second Street that morning. It must have been close to 5:00 A.M. And Big Jim Lawler had "invited" us to come back down to the Tenth Precinct at nine o'clock to go over things "while they're still fresh."

"Hey, Jim," I had protested, "did you ever hear of something called sleep?"

He had smirked. It was the only time he had looked at all pleased since we had woken him up.

Jennifer didn't even try to sleep. She took a shower, put on some coffee, and sat at the little table by the front window, brooding. I collapsed on the sofa and closed my eyes.

You know how it is when you try to take a catnap and you can't quite drop off? You know you have to sleep fast because you only have a short time, so you will yourself to sleep. You try every recipe you ever heard of. "Relax your feet . . . then your legs . . . then your torso . . . then your head." And your eyes open. Then you imagine a huge, black void, and try to immerse yourself deeper and deeper into it. And your eyes open. I tried all that, and through it all wound a faint melody that persisted in blipping along in the recesses of my mind. *Dum da dum, da dum, de dum . . .*

It didn't take long for panic to set in. Got to sleep . . . have to get up soon . . . have to . . . *Dum da dum, da dum, de dum* . . .

The panicky can't-sleep song that always torments me at such times is never a Brahms' symphony. It's always something like "You deserve a break today, so get up and get away, at McDonald's!" Open pop the eyes.

Then . . . *Dum da dum, da dum, Lucille* . . . Lucille? Where did that come from?

Where was that sleep that knits up the raveled sleeve of care? To sleep, perchance to dream? And who the hell is Lucille? And then my restless mind dug into some mysterious subconscious and found it for me. *Dum da, come with me, Lucille, dum-da-dum de Oldsmobile.*

There. Now I could sleep. It was the "Come with me, Lucille, in my merry Oldsmobile" song. And then my eyes *really* opened. I sat up. I blinked. Suddenly, it was 1793 Paris in the Place de la Revolution and a tumbrel was carrying a condemned traitor to the guillotine for crimes against humanity. Me.

I stood up. "Oh, Jupiter Optimus Maximus!" I muttered.

"What's the matter?" said Jennifer, looking over.

"The Auto Show!"

A great, molten, red-hot cannonball exploded through my brain, its roughly rounded form gradually assuming the image of Ironhead Matthews's contorted face. I remember pictures of ferociously scowling Burmese dragons on the walls of Oriental temples that looked like purring kittens by comparison.

I fairly leaped to the phone, and called the city desk. Del Brown, the lobster-desk man, answered.

"Hey, Del, it's Fitz."

"Up already?" he said cheerfully. "Or haven't you gone to bed?"

"Look, Del, was there an Auto Show slug on the schedule?"

"Ohhhhhhhh," he said. "Was that you?"

"Was what me?"

"The one Ironhead was ranting about."

"What did he say?"

"He called in after the circle replate and I thought somebody had shoved a red-hot poker up his grumper."

"What was he ranting about?" I asked hesitantly, not really wanting to know.

"No Auto Show story," Brown said casually. "He wanted to know if you had fallen into a hole."

"Oh."

"Or if you were hit by a taxi, or were in Bellevue in traction, or dead in the morgue."

The possible excuses for missing a story were thus offered.

"Is that all?"

"I think he left you a note," said Del, apparently totally indifferent to the fact that I was descending into a dungeon. "Oh, yes, here it is."

"What does it say?" I asked fearfully.

"Uh, well, it says, 'See me. Matthews.' "

" 'See me'?"

"That's it."

I hung up. "See me"! Only a reporter who has missed a story can understand the terror such innocent-sounding words can cause if they issue from a city editor.

I stumbled to the little coffee table and poured some coffee with trembling hands. There is no sin under the journalistic sky equal to missing a story. My mind, having finally alerted me with that goddamn Oldsmobile song, was now trying frantically to gear itself up to save me from Dr. Guillotine's infamous invention.

But Jennifer was on a totally different scent. "That man on the boat had to have something to do with this."

"What?"

"Why wouldn't he say who he was or what he was doing on the boat? We've got to find him."

"Listen," I plunged in, "you don't understand! I forgot to do an Auto Show story!"

That momentous pronouncement, I was certain, would galvanize her into action to save my life. I was wrong.

"We know what he looks like," she went on. "He should be easy to find."

I dug the Auto Show handout out of my pocket and scanned it frantically. Presten Morris was listed as the press agent. There were phone numbers for him at the Coliseum and at home. It was 7:00 A.M. I called him at home.

"Presten Morris?" I said into the phone.

"Yes."

"Hope I didn't wake you."

"Oh, no, I've been out jogging."

"Listen, this is Ed Fitzgerald of the *Daily Press.* . . ."

"Oh, yes! We were expecting you last night. I called your desk . . ."

"You called who?"

"Mr. Matthews at the city desk."

Wonderful, I thought. What would we do without press agents?

"Listen, I got delayed. I was shot dead at Bellevue Hospital."

"What? Shot?"

"It's okay. I'm all right. Look, I've got to interview that psychologist."

"Amanda Worth?"

"Yes."

"You mean *now*?"

"Yes!"

"Well," he said. "Well . . . maybe I can reach her and have her call you. Are you at the office?"

"No," I almost shrieked. "I'm home. Please have her call me here, okay?" I gave him the number.

"Well, okay," said Morris. "You want to come over and see the show?"

"Not tonight." I hung up.

"What am I going to tell Ironhead?" I muttered unhappily.

"Why do you call him Ironhead?"

"He got hit by a club during a riot one time. I think it regressed him until he's now a troglodyte."

I jumped into the shower and then shaved, trying to get myself functioning again. When I came back out, the psychologist, Amanda Worth, called from her home in Paramus, New Jersey. I interviewed her on the phone, sloughing off her questions about the peculiar hour I had chosen to talk to her. I managed to write a fast story on my typewriter about crazed male motorists fleeing down streets in their cars thinking of themselves as Sir Galahads slaying dragons.

When I called in with the story, I got Glenn, the nightside switchboard guy.

"Hey, Fitz," he said amiably. "What's doing?"

"Give me the desk," I said, torn between hoping Ironhead was there and wishing he were not. Del, the lobster editor, answered.

"Del," I said hesitantly, "is Ironhead in yet?"

"Any minute now. You want him?"

"No! Just tell him I filed an Auto Show story, will you?"

"Okay, Fitz."

I got Glenn to switch me to the wire room and started dictating the story.

Jennifer tapped me on the arm. "Fitz!"

I glanced up, trying to wake up, trying to concentrate, trying to keep annoyance out of my face. "What?"

"Fitz," she said, "do you think you could mention Daddy in the story?"

"In what story?"

"The Auto Show."

I looked at her blankly.

"Then you could run his picture."

I went back to dictating, wondering how I would survive Jennifer and Ironhead at the same time.

61

10

We WERE JUST about to leave my apartment for the Tenth Precinct to talk to Detective Lawler when the phone rang.

I'm not a superstitious person but sometimes when I consider Ironhead Matthews, the conception of reincarnation becomes attractive. It is entirely logical that Ironhead lived before—say in the Roman Empire in the person of the demented Emperor Caligula, who believed he had become a Roman god. Ironhead certainly doesn't consider himself an ordinary mortal—at least not when he's grilling one of his plebian reporters.

"What happened to the Auto Show story?" he was yelling at me over the phone on this particular headachy morning.

"I just phoned it in," I said hopefully.

"*Just*? You mean *now*!?"

"Well, see . . ."

"I sent you to the Coliseum last night, but where did you go?"

"I came across a better story, Ironhead . . ."

It's always a mistake to suggest even remotely that there can be a better story than the one you were sent to cover. Why a story is important is not always as obvious to you as it is to your city editor.

This was promptly explained to me through the medium of Mount St. Helens in full eruption. Spumes of clouds and ashes burst through the phone. I could imagine Ironhead's face turning into a cannonball.

Did I know that John McFadden, the publisher, was a car buff? Did I know he was up there at the Coliseum last night measuring and taking pictures of Mercedes and Audis and Rolls-Royces? Did I know he would be looking for an Auto Show story in today's paper? Did I know two and two? Did I know my grumper from second base at Yankee Stadium?

I had to admit across-the-board ignorance.

"So what the hell was this Pulitzer Prize story you went after instead of the Auto Show?" Ironhead demanded. It was clear it had better be the definitive answer to who erased the Nixon tapes or, at the very least, the documented inside story of who stole the French Connection heroin from police headquarters.

"You remember that murder on the Hudson River Cruises boat?" I started.

I could hear huffing and puffing. Ironhead was relighting his cigar and chewing it like a pirhana tearing the flesh off a goat.

" . . . the what . . .!"

"It's still unsolved," I said, but got no further.

Murders on the Hudson River or in Chelsea or on the Empire State Building or even in a goddam Chinese laundry were stories for Dubbs Brewer, the police reporter. "Dubbs is good at that," snapped Ironhead. "Dubbs is logical. He gets facts from the police. He doesn't go to the river and talk to the fish!"

The only safe words to say to Ironhead when he's lobbing artillery shells like that is "Yes, sir." So that's what I said.

"Don't get smart with me!" he yelled back.

I decided to be quiet.

How in the hell did I get lost on the way to the Auto Show? How in the goddamn hell did that lead to the Hudson River murder? How in the goddamn bitching hell did every assignment he sent me on turn into Dr. Livingstone getting lost in deepest Africa?

Wheels were meshing inside Ironhead's heated brain. Out came a jumbled flotilla of purple hyperbole.

"Get your ass in here," he snapped. "And I don't want to hear any more about that damned excursion-boat story. You are off that story. You got that?"

I glanced at Jennifer, who was watching with hopeful interest, imagining somehow that Ironhead and the *Daily Press* and I were all teaming up to solve the murder of her father.

"Do you mind if I work on it in my spare time?" I made the mistake of saying. "I sort of promised somebody."

"Spare time?" Ironhead raged, and apparently knocked something over, because he sputtered furiously and uttered several obscenities normally used only by drunken pressmen. "There is no such thing as spare time on this newspaper!"

I realized that I had made a poor choice of words. The proper choice, of course, was abject silence.

Ironhead was still stewing, though, because all of a sudden he couldn't help asking, "What in the hell did you find that turned your head into petrified rock?"

"See, we went looking for Humphrey Bogart at the Improv . . ."

"You went looking for *who*?"

"That didn't work out, but then this guy took a shot at me."

"A shot?"

"And that's when we found the dead body."

"You found a . . . *what*?"

"It was too late for the circle replate."

"Well, who the hell was it? Anybody important?"

"I don't know. I'm just going over to the Tenth Precinct to get some more on it."

"You are getting your calcified butt into this office," Ironhead howled. "What's this got to do with that boat murder?"

"Ironhead, I'm telling you, I don't know yet. Lawler doesn't know what this guy Harry Berg was doing there."

"Harry Berg?"

"That's what his ID said. You know him?"

Well, how a reporter could work in New York for as long as I had and know so little about anything was an absolute impenetrable mystery! Harry Berg had his thumb in every crooked deal in the Big Apple! And I had his dead body in my lap?

"I don't know how a dumb doofus like you falls over these things," Ironhead shouted. "Get over to the Tenth and find out what's going on."

"You said I was off the story."

"When are you going to learn to listen to me!"

Bang! Errrrrrrr . . .

11

YOU MIGHT THINK THAT learning the identity of at least one of the people who was trying to get money out of Howard Ritter would shed a little light somewhere. But instead of answering questions, it raised tantalizing new ones. What in the world was a guy like Harry Berg doing in Jennifer's apartment in the first place? How had Howard Ritter gotten mixed up with him?

From what Lawler told us and from clippings in the *Daily Press* library, the profile that emerged was of a kind of Jack Ruby nightclub owner who thought of himself as a big-shot operator. He owned the Zebra Club on West Forty-sixth Street between Eighth and Ninth Avenues. Berg paid off anybody necessary and gave generously to hospitals, churches, and political parties. There were a couple of shooting incidents in his past, and he'd been arrested a few times but never indicted or convicted. It was a fairly typical picture of a tough mug on the fringe of the rackets who lived with muscle and guts and had a large and generally unaccounted-for cash flow. Harry Berg was the kind of guy detectives would question when a tractor trailer truckload of Chivas Regal was hijacked on the Cross Bronx Expressway.

The three of us—Jennifer, Lawler, and I—sat in the squad room above West Twentieth Street, trying to make sense of things. It didn't help that none of us had had much sleep and that we were irritable and cranky.

"Was your father into gambling?" he started off.

"Gambling? No, I don't think so. Maybe the lottery once in a while. Why?"

Lawler took a deep breath, lighted a cigarette, and fiddled with a yellow pencil. "Berg had a couple of gambling clubs. He went to your apartment to collect money. Could it have been a gambling debt?"

Jennifer wagged her head over that. "My father—a fifty-thousand dollar gambling debt?" Her voice went way up on the last word, as though the mere suggestion were poppycock.

"There are a lot of show-business guys who get in over their heads."

"My father wouldn't even bet on pool games at the Players Club," Jennifer snorted. "He was terrified about money."

Lawler looked at her. "He needed money?"

She smiled innocently. "Doesn't everyone?"

"Well, do you have any idea why Harry Berg was at your apartment, then?" Lawler said, looking sideways at her.

"No, I don't," she said, "but it's got to have something to do with my father's death. Why don't you figure that one out? Then you'll know who got Berg."

"You think every crime in the city is connected to your father's death."

"The same person shot them both," said Jennifer. "And if you don't find him, I will!"

"That's what you were doing at that nightclub?" asked Lawler.

"Yes."

"And did you find somebody?"

"No." She sighed. "I thought I had, but we were all together the night Berg was killed, so it couldn't have been him."

"So will you please stop and let us handle this?" he said hopefully.

"Sure." She smiled. "As soon as you do something. Somebody paid my daddy two hundred bucks to deliver something to the riverboat. Do you know who that is yet?"

"No," Lawler admitted glumly. "Maybe he was delivering gambling money. Maybe instead of delivering it, he kept it."

"That's ridiculous," snapped Jennifer.

"Why?" Lawler countered.

"Because it is!"

"What would you like us to do?" he asked in annoyance.

"What about that man on the boat who wouldn't identify himself!" she said. "Did you ever get anything on him?"

Lawler smiled slyly. "Yes," he said, "we did. A lawyer out with a woman he wasn't married to. No connection."

The phone on Lawler's desk rang. He picked it up.

"Tenth Squad . . . Lawler." He listened. "Yeah, Fisk." He listened and leaned forward, making notes with his pencil. "Okay," he finally said, hung up, and looked at us.

"What?" I asked expectantly.

"Different weapon."

"What?" Jennifer chipped in.

"That was ballistics. Berg was killed with a .38. Your father with a nine millimeter."

"My God!" Jennifer gasped, her head reeling with images of an army of gunmen stalking the city. I didn't like it much either.

Lawler stood up. "We've got more checking to do. If you hear anything, let me know." He turned on me. "And I don't want to read any of this in the *Daily Press*."

"What?" I said, coming to attention.

"This is a confidential interrogation."

"I have to write *something*!"

"Stick to Berg, that's all. And nothing about the gun."

Jennifer was on her feet now too. "Stick to Berg? What about my father?"

Lawler sighed and rubbed his eyes. He looked at her.

"Listen, you want something in the paper about your father? Okay, the department's investigating his possible connection with Berg's gambling clubs. You want that in the paper?"

"No."

"Okay."

It was lovely. The two of them were figuring out what I was allowed to write. The only problem was that Ironhead wasn't there to get the word.

I drove Jenny across town to an ad agency on Third Avenue, where she was auditioning for a commercial about puppy food or something.

"Do you talk like a dog?" I asked.

She laughed. "Sometimes I'm a cat too." She reached over to squeeze my arm as I drove. "I told you actors do all kinds of voices."

I dropped her off and drove on down to the *Daily Press*. When I came into the city room, Ironhead spotted me and his face lighted up like the winner of the Irish Sweepstakes.

"Goddamn it, I never thought this piece of crap would ever amount to a decent story," he chortled. "But now you bring me Harry Berg on a platter! Beautiful! What the hell's the deal, anyway?"

"I wish I knew," I said guardedly.

Ironhead's face blew into a storm cloud. His forehead lowered as his cheeks puffed out into a pout. "You're inside the whole damn story, aren't you?" he challenged. "You got there when the body was still warm."

"Yeah, but I don't know what the hell Berg was doing there."

"Come here," said Ironhead, dragging me over to Arty Graves's desk on the rewrite battery. "Arty's writing a piece on it. You fill him in, and don't hold anything back to protect that broad."

"Arty?" I muttered. "I could write it."

"Goddamn it, you're practically a suspect," said Ironhead, his face getting red. "Give what you've got to Arty." He glared at Graves. "Make it sing, Arty, and keep your goddam Limey phrases out of it."

Ironhead stalked back to the city desk, slobbering over his cigar and already working himself up on how to handle the next story. I was still trying to cope with this turn of events when Arty smirked at me sideways and said, "Well, dear boy, I see you've got your tit in the wringer again." He seemed enormously pleased.

Well, I gave him everything I had, except that I played down the stuff about Lawler's suspicions of Howard Ritter's being a high-rolling gambler. My notes seemed to annoy him.

"What about the girl?" he asked in his loftily aristocratic manner, which he somehow thought was proper because he had once worked in Fleet Street in London. "Nobody cares about that lamentable actor."

"Listen, Berg was shot in Howard Ritter's apartment . . ."

"You mean in the bird's apartment . . ."

"And the two murders have got to be tied up . . ."

"What does the Ritter bird have to do with Berg?"

"Goddamn it, Arty . . ."

"Ironhead wants Harry Berg and the girl in this story."

What could you expect from a Goddamn know-it-all Limey who looks like Ashley Wilkes in *Gone With the Wind* and still thought of ink-stained wretches like me as colonial subjects?

"What do the cops say?" Ashley Wilkes wanted to know, and I filled him in as best I could on Berg. Of course, being a snoopy reporter, he kept coming back to the gambling angle.

"Was Berg down there trying to collect from that deadbeat actor? Maybe we could work that in."

"Listen, nobody knows why he was there."

Arty complained that the story was full of holes—which it was—and he couldn't turn in that load of salmagundi to Ironhead because Ironhead can't stand loose ends.

People think newspapers love really knotty mysteries, but that's a lot of crap. They like stories in which everything is known right away and the killer and the victim are both in the

Social Register or City Hall. What they want is Jean Harris the headmistress shooting Herman Tarnower the rich diet doctor and then telling a cop she did it.

The story had no Social Register, nobody with a smoking gun in his hand. We had dead bodies, all right—two of them. And weapons—two of them too. And suspects. Fourteen hundred on the boat alone, not to mention a bevy of comics who could all do Humphrey Bogart.

We had Ashley Wilkes's story too, over which I had no control but for which I would be blamed by everybody. When I added it all up, I decided I needed a drink.

12

I THINK IT WAS after the murder of Harry Berg that things got completely out of hand. Not that I was in control before that, but things hadn't been so hopelessly mixed up. For one thing, the story was all over the city. The damned radio guys got it out first, of course, and then TV got onto it. They were out with the story that afternoon before Ashley Wilkes's mishmash came out in the *Daily Press*. All about the murder of a shady nightclub operator in the Gramercy Park apartment of an off-Broadway actress whose father had been killed earlier under unexplained circumstances. The damned stories reeked with innuendo. And of course every damned detail that went out on the radio and television or was printed anywhere was blamed on me, personally, by Lawler and Jennifer.

Before the *Daily Press* even came out, Lawler was on the phone to me in the city room complaining that the story on the radio was all balled up.

"You guys make it sound as though we're not getting anywhere!"

"*Us* guys?" I mumbled. "I didn't tell the radio bunch anything."

"Don't you guys realize that anybody who's mixed up in this thing will go under cover now that all this stuff is all over the radio? Goddamn it!"

Then Jennifer called from her office. She had heard the radio too.

"Those stories make it sound like I knew Harry Berg," she complained.

That's what happens when a dead body turns up on your living-room rug, I explained.

"What am I going to do? I'm so tired! I feel like I've been awake for a month."

"Go to my place," I told her. "Get some sleep. Nobody will find you there."

I decided the place to have a drink was at the Zebra Club, lately owned by Harry Berg. I drove across to the West Side, parked in the West Forty-fourth Street NYP zone, and walked up to Forty-sixth Street. Lawler had told me Berg had a wife, Sylvia, who more or less ran the club while Harry was being a big shot.

"What did she say?" I had asked Lawler.

"She said nothing eight ways." He had smiled. "Her name ought to be Ice Berg."

The Zebra Club has a smart black-and-white-striped awning in front, and the outside is white like the walls of a Moroccan palace.

Sylvia Berg turned out to be what the fashion magazines called a monochromatic blonde. Her hair was blond and her skin was fair and she wore all white. The only different-colored things were large, round gold earrings, gold fingernails and toenails, green eyes, and a red mouth set in a firm, suspicious line.

She was sitting in a booth near the front door, adding up figures with a calculator and a slim golden pen, her eyes flitting constantly around the room, from the bar to the dining room to the piano bar. I walked over, and was caught in her Eveready eyes long before I got there.

"Yes?"

"Hi. Ed Fitzgerald. *Daily Press.*"

"What can I do for you?" She didn't introduce herself or

74

offer me a seat. She didn't blink or flinch or anything else either.

"May I sit down?" I ventured.

"Why not?" she said, nodding slightly. I slid into the booth and tried out a winsome smile. No luck, I was facing one of the stone dragons from Angkor Wat.

"I'm sorry to bother you, Mrs. Berg. I'm trying to find out anything I can about your husband's death."

That topic caused no ripple either. "I told everything to the police."

"Yes, I know. Lawler told me he'd talked to you. Did he ask you anything about money?"

Ice Berg's green eyes registered, at last. "Money?"

"Jennifer Ritter says he came to her apartment looking for money. Money he said her father had taken from him."

Sylvia took a long, slim, white cigarette from a case and lighted it with a lighter. "Yes, it seems to me I heard something about that."

I noticed that Sylvia's idea of an answer was quaint.

"Do you know anything about Ritter getting money from your husband?"

"I told the police what I know, which is nothing."

"So you don't know if any money is missing?"

Sylvia Berg puffed on her cigarette and looked straight ahead. "If Harry went looking for money, I guess there was money missing."

"Was it money from his gambling clubs?"

"Gambling clubs?"

I sighed. "The police say he had a couple of gambling clubs, and that's about the only place I can think of where he'd come up with fifty thousand in cash."

She actually looked at me then. "Fifty thousand dollars? Where did you get that figure?"

"Ritter's daughter, Jenny, said that's how much he was looking for."

Sylvia Berg's decorative mouth went into a rigid, straight

75

line, and her lips pursed. She shook her head in annoyance. "The fool!" she said bitterly.

"He never reported any money stolen to the police?" I said.

"Harry wouldn't go to the police."

"No. Because the money was from gambling, right? The police think Howard Ritter ran up fifty thousand in gambling debts."

Ice Berg smirked at me and shook her head in wonder at my naïveté. "If Harry did run gambling clubs, and I'm not saying he did, he certainly wouldn't allow anybody that kind of credit."

I had to think that was the truth, actually. It made sense. Ritter had to be a delivery boy.

"Did Ritter work for your husband?"

"I have no idea," she said.

"Could he have been delivering money for him from his clubs?" I asked. "If there are any clubs, that is."

Sylvia shrugged. "I don't know. Never heard the name until after . . ."

"Did your husband drink white wine?"

"Yes. Sometimes."

"Not especially?"

"No. Usually Scotch. Why?"

"Somebody was hiring Ritter to deliver wine to him. Did your husband ever call himself Mr. Goodman?"

Sylvia shook her head at that. "Not that I know of." She studied me for a moment. "Harry was a fool about money, you know," she volunteered. "He was a big shot, of course. All you had to do was ask him, and he'd tell you he was. But money went through his hands like water."

Apparently the gambling clubs and the cash they generated had been a sore point with her.

"You're looking for a story, Fitzgerald? Is that it? Well, if it's about Harry, look for a girl."

"Any particular girl?"

"No," she said cynically. "Harry wasn't too particular."

─────13─────

WHEN I GOT HOME to East Eighty-second Street that night, Jennifer was sleeping like a hibernating bear. I was thoroughly exhausted too, but in that restless condition in which you can't sleep. I stretched out in the bathtub with Marcus Aurelius, looking for some serenity from his *Meditations*. This was the message I got from the Roman emperor-philosopher whom I had come to think of as my mentor and guru:

"This is the chief thing: Do not be perturbed, for all things are according to the laws of nature; and in a little time you will be nobody and nowhere; like Hadrian and Augustus."

So much for Marcus on this occasion. Don't be perturbed? Obviously he had never had to deal with life in the Big Apple. I put Marcus aside and slid deeper down into the water.

It's odd but sometimes the more information you get about something, the more confusing it becomes. You keep trying to arrange things into a logical sequence. Inside my inflamed mind a game of ticktacktoe was before me. If I could only get a row of *X*s or *O*s lined up in order, maybe I could solve things. Howard Ritter and Harry Berg were hopping around on the edges of the game, tossing $50,000 back and forth. Big Jim Lawler was there too, like a referee. "Maybe Ritter was delivering money for Berg and decided to keep it," he had suggested.

77

Okay. Ritter delivers money for Berg, but takes $50,000 home instead. One X. Berg goes after his money, and somebody kills him. Two Xs. Whoever shot Berg, it couldn't have been Ritter. He was already dead. It couldn't have been Jennifer, because she was with me, and that was nonsense anyway. So who was it? Where was the third X?

I tried Os. Now Berg is Mr. Goodman. One O. He hires Ritter to deliver money for him. Two Os. Ritter steals the money and goes on board the Hudson River Cruises boat with it, where somebody kills him. Is that a third O, or is it an X? Some game.

One thing finally became clear, though. I kept coming back to Ritter. He was hired to make deliveries for Mr. Goodman. That could be Berg. One X. He goes on board the boat. Why? I couldn't even get past the first X until I figured that one out.

I had the most awful nightmares that night, all full of boat whistles and dancing Os dressed in orange sweaters and Xs in white monochromatic suits. I woke up as grumpy and out of sorts as a Parris Island drill sergeant receiving a new busload of raw recruits.

Jennifer was up and gone. I was about as low as I could get on the Ritter murder. The *Daily Press* was on the little table, full of the story. Lawler was right about that too. Anybody involved would be burrowing into a hole when he saw that.

That day at the office, Jim Owens told me Father Callahan was out sick, and I was being sent down to Manhattan State Supreme Court for the day to fill in. Tom Callahan is tall, slim, and collegiate-looking, and he's so polite that somebody said he must have come out of a seminary. So, everybody calls him Father Callahan.

I didn't mind. It would keep me busy for the day and get my mind off that damnable ticktacktoe game. I had covered the court down at Foley Square in one of my earlier incarnations at the *Daily Press*, and when I got there I received a big greeting from Harry Reeves, the *Post* reporter.

"Well, if it isn't Fitzboggin." He chortled. He called me that because, he once explained, all Irishers are out of the peat bogs.

I hopped around the immense old museum of a place checking on show-cause orders and damage suits, and found myself dashing to the elevator from the county clerk's office in the basement. I just managed to slide in, and turned around to face the front. Something flitted across my mind.

The elevator rose slowly to the first floor, where most of the people got off. I glanced around at a man who was still in the car. He was looking ahead, minding his own business. I looked at him again. Bushy moustache and tight curly hair. "Lawyer," a voice inside my head told me.

The elevator started up again. My mind was nudging me about the moustache. Naturally, he would be a lawyer, here in a courthouse. So what? The doors opened on the third floor, and he walked out. I followed, tugged along by I still didn't know what. He walked into Part Five, otherwise known as Divorce Court.

I peeked into Part Five. The moustache walked up into the front well of the court and sat down at a lawyers' table beside a washed-out-looking man in a brown-striped summer suit. A client, no doubt. I was about to leave, when I happened to look at the other counselor's table. There sat the lavender lady I had seen on the riverboat the day Ritter was murdered. One more glance at the moustache and I had it. The lawyer who refused to identify himself. I slid into the court and eased onto a bench.

In a few minutes, roly-poly Judge Nacht waddled out, climbed onto the judge's bench, and called the divorce proceedings to order. In a twinkling it all became clear, as Stegman v. Stegman unfolded.

The lavender lady was Eva Stegman and her husband was Walter Stegman. Moustache the lawyer was representing Walter Stegman. How simply beautiful! He was representing the husband in a divorce action but romancing the wife. No wonder he didn't want anybody to know he and Eva had been on their way to Bear Mountain together for a picnic. And Lawler had told me Moustache was married too. All of a sudden the canon of legal ethics flip-flopped and I was the Grand High Executioner.

I waited around until there was a break in the testimony, and then went up to the court clerk and got Moustache's name. Stuart Kravitz. When I went out into the corridor, he was standing with his fidgety client by the water fountain.

"Counselor," I said to him, "excuse me. I have a message for you from the appellate division."

Kravitz looked at me in surprise, but walked along behind me through the hallway leading to the circular balcony around the great rotunda.

"Yes?" he said when I stopped and faced him.

"Ed Fitzgerald. *Daily Press*."

Kravitz frowned and looked confused. "This case is nothing," he smiled.

"Counselor," I went on, "it's about the Hudson River Cruises excursion boat."

Like the fixed smile on a wax doll when you put it too near a fire, Kravitz's plastered-on grin melted and slid downward into a frown, and then into a pugnacious grimace.

"What about it?" he said curtly.

"Counselor, all I'm looking for is some help, if you can give it to me. You were on board when a man was killed."

Kravitz's face went violently red, and he recoiled as though stricken by the fangs of a cobra. "Who said so?" he snapped.

"I know so," I said. "If you make me prove it, it'll wind up in the paper."

Stu Kravitz edged forward, bringing his face close to mine. He was livid, his mouth quivering. "Now, you listen here, whatever your name is . . ."

"Fitzgerald."

"Fitzgerald. I satisfied every legal requirement. I didn't identify myself because I was in no way involved."

"Then why the big cover-up?"

"I don't have to stand here . . ." He glared at me. "There was no cover-up. I exercised my constitutional rights."

"Mr. Kravitz, take it easy. All I'm trying to find out is if you saw anything unusual on the boat that day."

"You're mistaken. I wasn't on any boat!"

"You were on the boat, all right. And you were with Eva Stegman. She's right outside the courtroom door. Shall I ask her?"

Kravitz trembled and backed off. "This is not what it appears," he finally said softly.

"It's not?"

"No."

"What it appears is that Stuart Kravitz, attorney-at-law, is representing Walter Stegman in a divorce case and at the same time romancing Walter's wife, Eva," I said. "I'm glad that's not what it is."

"I am not romancing her."

"Then you wouldn't mind if I showed a photo of the two of you together to Judge Nacht?"

Stu Kravitz's flushed face went pale and he leaned back against the wall outside Divorce Court. He muttered or gurgled something about coercion or maybe blackmail.

"How about ethics, Kravitz? Ever hear of them?"

"Look, I told you I don't know anything. So we were on the boat together. That's all."

"Counselor, for God's sake, don't you realize a man was killed? All I want is for you to tell me if you saw anything. Or if Mrs. Stegman saw anything."

Kravitz took my arm and practically dragged me out onto the marble balcony that circles the great rotunda. "I've never done anything like this before," he said.

"Did you see anything at all?" I pressed.

Kravitz rubbed his face, trying to stir up memories. "I don't know. Nothing! We were on the deck above."

"You were right above it?"

"I don't know. Yes, I guess so. There was just the river. Boats! That's all. Listen, I have to get back."

"There were other boats around?"

"Yes. There was one, anyway. A cabin cruiser."

"Where was it?"

"Behind us."

Kravitz paced anxiously away to look back down the corridor toward Divorce Court, and then hurried back. "If they found out!" he muttered.

"Was the cruiser following the excursion boat?" I asked.

"I don't know. It was there. When that bag fell overboard, the cruiser picked it up. I remember that now."

"What?"

"I remember now the cruiser fished something out of the water."

"Something that fell from the riverboat?"

"Yes."

"What was it?"

"Something red. A bag or something."

"You mean the bag floated until the cruiser got to it?"

"Yes, I guess it did."

"Did the cruiser keep on coming and return it to whoever dropped it, do you know?"

"No, the excursion boat kept going. The cruiser pulled the red bag from the water and turned back. Now, that's absolutely all I know."

"What about Mrs. Stegman?"

"No, no. She wasn't looking that way. She was looking at me. Are you going to tell anybody about us?"

I studied his face. Desolation and out-of-control fright.

"Should I?"

He watched me in silent appeal. If the bar association heard about this, Stuart Kravitz could be censured, suspended—maybe disbarred. In the face of that, I believed he had told me all he knew.

"What kind of representation is your client getting in this case, counselor?" I asked.

Kravitz leaned back against a marble column and closed his eyes. "I'll withdraw as counsel," he breathed softly. "I'll withdraw."

I walked away. Howard Ritter's death was still causing ripples. Riding down on the elevator, my mind was no longer conjuring with Xs and Os. It was fixed on the image of a red bag floating in the Hudson. Miss Grady at Actors Equity had told us that somebody had left Howard Ritter a "red thing . . . like something you take to the beach." Something that floated.

14

IDON'T REMEMBER WHAT I covered the rest of that day at the courthouse. I walked around in a daze, playing ticktactoe inside my head one minute and thinking about the floating red bag the next.

"Hey, Fitzboggin," Harry complained, "come up for air."

"Huh?"

Ritter had gone aboard the riverboat before 10:00 A.M. the day he was killed. One *X*. Okay, where was he coming from? If Harry Berg were the mysterious Mr. Goodman, then Ritter could have been coming from the Zebra Club. Two *X*s. Was he delivering money for Harry Berg? If so, to whom? The way it was adding up, Ritter went on board the riverboard, put that money into the inflatable red bag, and dropped it off the stern. The question was, did he drop it off on purpose? Or did it fall when somebody shot him? Or did he throw it over the stern to keep it away from whoever was about to shoot him?

"Your fly's open," Harry Reeves told me while we were in Special Term, Part One, listening to a hearing.

"Who could have been in that cabin cruiser?" was my answer.

"Go back to sleep," said Reeves.

I remained fogbound the rest of the day as my mind chased an elusive plan sliding along just below the surface of my consciousness like a great spouter whale. Finally, I realized what it was. If I retraced Ritter's movements—or what I speculated were his movements—maybe I could find someone who had seen something that morning.

The Zebra Club wasn't open the next morning when I walked up to the door at about nine-thirty, which I figured was about the latest Ritter could have gotten there and still have made the river boat at ten.

I had to bang on the large wooden door with a chapel arch. A shadow loomed up behind the glass, and then somebody harrumphed something, and I heard him clunking on the door. Then it opened.

A slim, weathered, red-faced Hispanic man looked out, squinting into the sun. "Sí . . . yes?" he said blinking.

"Anybody here?" I said rather idiotically.

"Yes?"

"Can I come in?" I said, moving to open the wooden door. The guy apparently was a porter, and used to letting in anyone who demonstrated authority. He stood aside, and I walked across the red-tile floor into the bar area. The high-backed wooden stools were leaned against the oak bar.

"Nobody here," the porter was saying to me. "Fi . . . ten minutes."

"Who will be here in ten minutes?"

"Mr. Fields. Bartender," he said, gesturing uncertainly and giving me a fawning smile.

Maybe he knew something. "Do you remember a man coming here one morning with a red bag to pick up something?" I asked him.

"Mr. Berg not here," he smiled.

"Yes, yes, I know."

"Mrs. Berg tonight."

"How long have you worked here?" I tried again.

"Three day."

"Was there a porter here before that?" I asked.

"Left," the man said and shrugged.

That stopped me. It was the kind of thing I was looking for. Something unusual. At about the same time Ritter was murdered, somebody quit his job.

"You know who he is?" I asked.

"No, I don't think so," the porter said, looking at the floor.

"I'm not the police," I said. "I need to find him." I took out a twenty-dollar bill and held it out.

"Manny Torres," he said immediately. "Emanuel Torres. New Jersey." He took the twenty.

"Where in New Jersey?"

"You wait," he said, and went behind the bar. He picked up a small notebook and found the address. "Kennedy Boulevard, West New York," he said. "Seventeen twenty-one."

I was about to leave when a key turned in the front door, and in walked a large, young, handsome man with a bow tie and alert eyes. The eyes settled on me at once.

"Can I help you?" he said in a take-charge voice. "I'm the day bartender here."

The porter smiled and backed away like an Oriental servant.

"Were you here the morning Howard Ritter showed up?" I asked, deciding to jump forward a square and see what might happen.

The day bartender walked along the bar and went back behind it, apparently giving himself time to think. He leaned over the bar at me. "No. I came in just afterward."

"Do you know what happened?"

"Only what Harry said. That he'd been robbed. Mrs. Berg came in, and that's what he told her."

I tried to keep a calm face when he said that. Robbed? Ritter robbed Berg that morning? My ticktacktoe game went into overtime.

"Did he say how much was taken?" I finally managed.

The bartender shook his head. "Not that I heard."

"Did he describe the bandit?"

"Yeah. About forty-five or fifty. Average height. Wore a

sport jacket. Had a little fringe of a beard around his chin. I already gave a statement."

That sounded like Howard Ritter, all right.

"You with Midtown North?" he asked.

"Midtown North? I'm with the *Daily Press*. Ed Fitzgerald."

Fields's face went hard and white, and he straightened up and glared at me. "What? Whyn't you tell me?"

"You didn't ask."

I walked out into the warming sun and followed my nose to an outside phone booth on Eighth Avenue. But there was no phone listed for an Emanuel Torres on Kennedy Boulevard or anyplace else in West New York. I walked to my car, climbed in, and headed down Ninth Avenue. Down to Thirty-seventh Street and then west down into the entrance of the Lincoln Tunnel to New Jersey.

The Falcon sputtered and coughed, making the long, curving climb out of the tunnel and up the steep concrete highway. You go over a ridge along the Hudson River, and then down again into the row of little cities along the river. West New York, New Jersey, is one of those unnoticed blue-collar towns that make up the urban sprawl just across the Hudson from New York City. Through the middle of it is Kennedy Boulevard, a wide street with sagging wooden buildings on both sides and the look of a midwestern town in the 1950s. A lot of the Irish have moved out, and a Cuban community has replaced them.

I found Manny Torres's address, but no Manny. I knocked on the apartment door next to it in the two-story frame tenement with asphalt shingles. Somebody pulled back the curtains and peered out.

"Torres?" I said. "I'm looking for Manny Torres."

"*No hablo ingles*," the shadowy woman called out, and the curtains swung back behind the door.

I walked along the street a few doors, and saw clothes hung out to dry on the lines between the buildings. There were rows and rows stretching for a block of lines festooned with chil-

88

dren's pajamas and shirts. On the corner I saw a small bar named Los Muchachos with a CERVEZA sign in the window. I walked into the comfortable gloom.

There was a small pool table beside the bar and a red-and-yellow illuminated juke box that was blaring away with salsa music. The pool players were black or Hispanic, and so were the three regulars at the end of the bar.

"Yes," the barmaid said, moving over to where I had taken a stool.

"Hot day," I said, trying to establish a little rapport. "You got Schaefer?"

"No," she said.

"Budweiser."

She brought it and gave me a glass. The regulars were glancing at me, and the pool players looked around every so often too. I don't know if it's because I'm Irish or because I'm a reporter or maybe both, but many people take me for a cop on first glance. I sipped the Budweiser and figured that unless I stayed there several hours, there wasn't much chance of my establishing rapport.

"Listen," I said, "I'm a reporter. *Daily Press.*" Almost nobody ever asks a reporter to see his press card, but in this case I took it out of my jacket pocket and put it on the bar in front of the barmaid. She picked it up, examined the photograph on it, which makes me look like a minor Romanian customs clerk, and smiled.

"Great picture," I said, and she laughed a little. "Listen, I'm trying to find a guy who lives around the corner. Manny Torres. There's nothing wrong, I just want to talk to him about a story. You know where I can find him?"

The three regulars were slowly moving over to stand by us. The barmaid showed them my press card, which was working like a passport in this foreign enclave. They stared at me, but they seemed friendly enough. I ordered drinks for them all, and put some money in the glowing yellow jukebox. I pushed a button and got "Pedro Navaja."

"I don't know what it means," I said, "but it's lively."

The barmaid laughed. " 'Peter the Knife,' it means. He's a peemp. He tries to use his knife on his girl, and she shoots him."

"Nice song," I said.

"It's true," she smiled.

I sat on the barstool and sipped the Budweiser. "I'm trying to find Manny Torres to see why he quit his job," I said. "Anybody know him?"

They smiled and drank and I set up another round. One of the regulars went to a phone and made a call, glancing at me. In fifteen minutes, another man walked into Los Muchachos, and I knew it was Torres.

The one who had made the phone call went over to the new arrival and whispered to him. Torres looked at me and then came and sat on the stool next to mine.

"What do you want with Torres?" he said. He was dark and thick, with a moustache and skin the color of shoe leather, and his flowered shirt hung down over his trousers.

"I'm doing a story on a man who owned the Zebra Club in New York," I said, and felt a tremor go through the little group. "Somebody killed him."

"I read about that," one of the regulars said.

"Manny Torres worked for the guy, and he quit the other day, and I'm trying to find him."

Emanuel Torres shook his head and grunted and looked at me. *"No conto! Me votaron!"* he said.

"He didn't quit, he was fired," one of the others explained.

"Are you Manny Torres?" I asked.

"Yes."

"Harry Berg fired you?" I asked.

Torres flushed angrily. "Yes, for no good reason. Too bad he got shot," he added sarcastically.

"Were you there when Berg was robbed?"

"Yes, I was," said Torres. "I see the whole thing."

I told the barmaid to set up another round of drinks. Torres took a gulp and continued. Harry was in his office with the door closed, as usual, that morning. "When he counts his money in the morning, he close the door. He think I don't know about that," said Torres.

"What money?"

"Money. *Mucho dinero.* From his clubs. *El es muy jugador!* Big gambler."

On that morning, he said, Berg had suddenly flung the office door open and walked out to look around anxiously.

"I see *dinero* stacked up on his desk," he said. "He tell me, 'Look out for some man coming in.' Then he get some bottles of wine and some ice."

Torres had gone to the front of the club and watched the street, but he could also see Harry Berg. "He go in his office and put money in a bag, and then he cover it with the wine bottles and the ice."

"He covered the money up with wine?" I asked.

"Ice all over it, and bottles."

In a few moments there had been a knock on the club door, and Torres let in the middle-aged man in the sport coat and with the little beard. He walked to Harry's office, and Harry came out with the bag of wine, ice, and money.

"The man take the bag and put that bag into a bag he has—a red bag," said Manny. "Then he go out."

"Didn't he say anything?"

"Just that he is supposed to pick up something."

"Didn't Harry say anything?"

"No."

"Nothing at all?"

"No. *Nada.* Not a word."

I looked at him in confusion. "That's a robbery?"

Torres cocked his head to one side, indicating agreement that it was strange.

"The man didn't show a gun or anything?"

"No. Just walk in, take the bag, walk out."

"Do you know if Harry had a gun?" I asked.

"Yes," he nodded energetically. "He shot people before!"

Odd, I thought. A tough nut like Harry Berg lets a soft guy like Howard Ritter take money without a struggle.

"Do you remember anything else?"

Torres shook his head back and forth slowly, apparently reviewing it all in his mind. "When his wife come in later, he tell her he is robbed."

It certainly seemed to be a peculiar robbery.

"Mrs. Berg, she asked him, 'Why you don't shoot him?' He say he is too surprised." Manny grimaced sarcastically. "Then he look at me and close the office door. I hear her yelling his head off."

"What was she saying?"

"Oh, she don't believe him, about being robbed. She scream she want that money back."

"And then he fired you?" I asked.

"He say he has to let me go because business is no good," said Manny, "but that is not reason. Is because I hear him yell out his girlfriend's name and because I know robbery was something funny. He was afraid I tell his wife—or maybe the cops."

"What's this?" I interrupted. "He called his girlfriend's name?"

"Oh, I don't tell you that? *Sí*, when he is in the office and he open the door, he has the telephone in his hand and he yell, 'Taffy!' That's his girl."

"Was she on the phone?"

He shrugged. "I guess so. That's all he say."

"Who's Taffy?"

Taffy, said Torres, is a dancer who worked at the Zebra Club until Sylvia Berg noticed what was going on, and then Taffy was out. "But he still going around with her anyway. So he fire me and gave me a big hundred bucks. But Manny Torres isn't so dumb as that. I get another five hundred from Mrs. Berg later."

"How'd that happen?"

"Because she call me up at my sister's and ask me about that robbery. I tell her how Mr. Berg say 'Taffy' on the phone."

I sat there over my Budweiser in Los Muchachos listening to the blaring salsa music and hearing the click of pool balls and pondering it all. The more I heard about what happened at the Zebra Cub, the more confusing it became. A robbery that wasn't a robbery. Money hidden under wine bottles and ice. And now Taffy.

"You know where I could find this Taffy?" I asked.

"Forty-second Street," he said.

"Where on Forty-second Street?"

"Not on—in. She's in the show."

15

B Y THE TIME I drove back down through the Lincoln Tunnel and across Manhattan to the *Daily Press*, it was almost two in the afternoon.

Ironhead glowered and said, "Thanks for coming in, Fitz. Do you know what time it is?"

"Sorry," I said. "Checking out something on the Harry Berg story."

"Oh, yeah, where—Alaska?"

"New Jersey."

Ironhead's jaw began working, and I could see he didn't know whether he wanted to ask any more about that or not. Finally, he couldn't stand it. "Why Jersey?"

"Well, see, they fired the first porter, just like that. So, I wondered why?"

"Porter?"

"At the Zebra Club. So I found him in West New York, and he says Berg had a girlfriend."

Ironhead studied my face as though searching for traces of insanity. "Harry Berg had a girl, huh?" He sneered. "Well, that's a helluva scoop. I want you to let Dubbs watch that story. I've got a nice little feature for you. See Owens."

On my desk I found a message from Danny the switchboard guy that somebody named Max Kasian had called. It didn't mean anything to me.

Jim Owens, the assistant city editor, gave me a handout about a big-deal art auction at Sotheby's and I was supposed to write something cute about a $4 million oil painting bought by some anonymous collector. I always wondered what kind of people had $4 million for a painting in a world of out-of-work porters. I sat there looking at the handout and at a photograph of the painting, which was of a fat woman, a thin dog, and a lemon rind. Not surprisingly, my attention strayed to Taffy and *42nd Street*.

Finally, I called backstage at the theater and asked the man who answered if there were a girl named Taffy in the show.

"We don't give out no information about the dancers," he said flatly, and hung up. Another lovely person brightening my day.

That night I hung around the stage door, which is around in back in an alley off Forty-fifth street. You walk through a covered alley and turn left along another one, and there are the stage doors of the Royale, the Golden, and the Majestic. Gypsies and actors were streaming in through the alley for all three shows. The female dancers were all pale-faced and wrapped up in jeans and old shirts and looked like teenage Central Park dog walkers.

"Has Taffy gone in yet?" I asked one girl.

"I don't know," she said and kept walking.

"Do you know Taffy?" I asked another one, and she gave me a look, smiled, and didn't stop either. Being a Stage Door Johnny was hard work.

After that, I just stood there and said, "Taffy?" as each dancer came by. Some didn't even look, and a few shook their heads.

But finally my call of "Taffy" brought a response as a diminutive brunette halted and looked at me. "Yes?" she said in a melodious little voice.

"Listen," I said, stepping closer. "Can I talk to you? I'm with the *Daily Press*. Ed Fitzgerald."

Taffy smiled at that. "What do you want, an interview?" she said ingenuously, flashing a smile that demolished me.

"Yes," I said. "Could you meet me after the show?"

"Well," she said, looking me over. "Are you really a reporter?"

I took out my press card and showed her my rogues gallery photograph. She examined it and handed it back. I seemed to be showing it more in one day than I usually do in a year.

"Do you write about Broadway?" she wanted to know.

"Sometimes," I said. "Where could we meet?"

"Well," she said hesitantly, "right here, I guess. Ten-fifty, about." And then she flashed another heart-melting smile and ran in through the stage door.

I realize it was sort of a rotten trick to let her think I was interviewing her about her performing, but I had to find out about her and Harry Berg and that peculiar robbery.

I walked across Forty-fifth Street to the Theatre Bar to kill some time, and found Angie Pinzino at the end of the bar talking animatedly with a guy and a girl. I recognized them from the nightclub Going Up. The guy was Barney Wells, the fast-talking emcee with the gold chain and blown-back hair, and the girl was the waitress who had described him to us as "the funniest man in New York."

I walked down the bar and sat beside them. Angie stuck a piece of paper in front of me. "Whaddya think?" he beamed. I looked at the photograph of a Staten Island ferryboat.

"A ferryboat?" I asked stupidly.

Angie laughed, and put a beer in front of me. "Wrong!" He laughed. "A nightclub."

"Yeah?" I said, looking again. The ferryboat was called the Mae Murray.

"Yeah," said Angie. "After we buy her at auction from the city. How's it sound? Angelo Pinzino, maitre d'! And Barney's the entertainment."

I looked at Barney. He was beaming. He wore a powder-blue shirt open down to Greenwich Village, tight jeans, and some kind of yellow boots with high heels.

"You work at Going Up, right?" I ventured.

Barney's face sort of twitched. "Right," he said. "I used to, anyway. This is Joyce." He nodded toward his waitress girl-friend, who was sitting next to him, vacant-eyed. She looked spaced out.

"You've got to get your own place," Angie was saying. "That's what Barney keeps saying, and he's right. I got to get out of this falling-down dump."

"That's why I quit Vergari at Going Up," said Barney. "You've got to get your own place."

I lifted my Schaefer. "Good luck," I said.

"Oh, it's gonna be something." Angie laughed, taking the photograph back and devouring it with his lively dark eyes.

I looked at Barney, and it occurred to me that he might be able to help me find Humphrey Bogart. "Say, Barney, do you know any comic who worked at the Zebra Club?"

Barney studied me a moment. "Sure," he said. "I worked there myself once."

"Yeah? As a comic?"

"Right. Berg didn't know zip about comedy, though."

"He means he fired him," said Joyce hollowly, and laughed a faraway laugh. Barney gave her a black look.

"Aren't you the guy who told Trigger Moran you were going to put him in a show?" Barney finally said, looking back at me.

I'm afraid I blushed at that. "Oh, yeah," I confessed.

Angie Pinzino's dark eyebrows went up. "You're the one?" he said, surprised. He laughed. "You're Dave Kingman?"

"In left field," I said lamely.

Angie was still guffawing. "Trigger was checking the phone book like a maniac and screaming at his agent to find you! Boy, you did a job on him."

"What are you—a cop?" Barney asked.

"Naw. I'm with the *Daily Press*. Ed Fitzgerald."

"What are you digging into?"

I sighed. How to explain that? "Well, Barney, I'm trying to find a Mr. Goodman."

Barney frowned. "Goodman?"

"Or a comic who can do Humphrey Bogart."

He smiled. "Hell, anybody can do Bogart."

"So I found out. Any other comics work for Berg that you know of?"

Barney looked at Angie, and they both seemed to get the idea together. Barney looked back at me. "Trigger did."

"Yeah? What'd he do for Berg?"

Barney seemed reluctant to say more, but finally he said, "He worked at one of his after-hours joints."

"Yeah," said Angie. "He had some kind of a run-in with him, as a matter of fact."

"What kind of a run-in?"

"I never got it straight. Trigger wouldn't talk about it. But they roughed him up. He used to make deliveries for Berg."

"What kind of deliveries?"

"Well, he told us it was money," said Barney.

That interested me very much. I lit a Tiparillo. "He delivered money for Berg? Where?"

Angie scratched his chin and tried to think. "Now, I think he said he would take it from the after-hours joints to the Zebra."

"How much money would he carry, do you know?"

Angie smiled. "Well, I'll tell you. At first he said it was a few grand. Then it was five hundred grand . . . and then millions." He laughed. Then he leaned over the bar closer to me. "I think one of the deliveries came up short, you know?"

"Moran lifted some?"

Angie leaned back and cocked his head eloquently. Then he winked. "All I know is somebody worked Trigger over, and he didn't make any more deliveries."

I sat there puffing on the Tiparillo and tried to fit that into the picture. Moran had been forcibly retired from making deliveries for Harry Berg. Had Ritter taken over for him? Had Ritter been picking up money or pulling a robbery that day he was shot? Clearly, weasel Moran had some questions to answer. But at the moment it was time to talk with Taffy. I hurried back across the street to the stage door.

Taffy came jumping out right on time, and she looked even better than when she'd gone in. "Where shall we go?" she asked pertly.

"I don't care," I said. "You know a place?"

"Sure," she said, "come on," and led me over to Eighth Avenue and up to Broadway Joe's on West Forty-sixth, a few doors away from the Zebra Club. Broadway Joe's has an immense painted mural of movie and stage stars covering one side wall. Everybody from John Garfield to Vivien Leigh. When we were inside and at a little table by the mural, Taffy smiled again.

She wanted nothing but a Perrier. I ordered a Schaefer and examined Taffy's lovely little face. She was quite small, a miniature Venus, with a delicate porcelain face and eyes of deepest blue.

"What kind of a name is Taffy?" I asked.

She giggled. "Oh, it's just a nickname. Sally Taliferro! They started calling me Taffy in high school and it stuck."

"Where was high school?"

"Kansas City! Ever been there?"

I said I hadn't, but it sounded like a nice place.

"So, what do you want to ask me about?" she purred.

"Harry Berg."

Taffy stopped purring. She blinked those deep eyes, looked away and then back. "Oh, my God!" she whimpered, and I thought she was going to cry.

"I'm sorry," I said. "I'm trying to find out what happened to him."

Taffy sat there, unmoving, pale and looking like a scared kid. I wondered if she would ever speak again, but finally she looked up. "Are you a confidence man?" she asked in a tiny voice.

"Am I a what?"

"Do you believe in confidence?"

"You mean you want to tell me something in confidence?"

"Somebody told me that if you tell a reporter something and he agrees to be a confidence man, then he can't ever tell what you've said to a living soul!"

"Uh-huh," I hedged. "Well . . . that's true. Depending on what it is, of course."

"You have to promise," she said, and all of a sudden she was crying.

"Take it easy, Miss . . ."

". . . because I don't know what to do! And somebody has to help me! Because I did what I was supposed to, and I kept quiet, but I didn't know she was going to shoot him!"

"Wait a minute, Taffy. Who shot who?"

"Are you a confidence man?" she asked plaintively.

"Well . . ."

"All right, then. I'll walk out."

"Okay, okay. You can tell me in confidence."

"And you'll never tell a soul!"

"No."

"Not even the cops!"

Oh, Jupiter Optimus Maximus, I thought. What have I promised here?

"All right. Not even the cops. What's this all about?"

She blurted out that she was crazy with worry, and she knew the cops would catch up with her sooner or later. "If somebody else doesn't get me first!" And now she knew it would happen, because I had found her and that meant the police would too. "Because they're a lot smarter than mere reporters."

"I'm sorry to be a bother," I said. "Suppose you tell me what it's all about."

"I don't know how you can help me," she said quietly. "The one thing you must not do is even mention me!"

"Uh-huh," I mumbled.

"Do you always do that?" she pounced.

"What?"

"Say 'Uh-huh' when you don't want to answer?"

"Is that what I do?"

The waitress brought Taffy's Perrier and my Schaefer, and my little gypsy fell silent until we were alone again. She sipped her water and examined my face painstakingly, as though trying to commit it to memory or read its capacity for veracity. Staring into the face of a strikingly beautiful girl usually makes me extremely nervous. I blinked. Then I cleared my throat. Then I plunged in.

"What was that you said about somebody shooting somebody?"

Taffy put her glass down and looked down at the table. Then she glanced up at me. "How was I to imagine she would shoot him?" she said in a semiwhisper.

"Who?"

"Harry!"

"Harry Berg?"

Taffy nodded, as though unable to even voice his full name out loud.

"Who shot Harry?" I asked softly.

"His wife, of course!"

I leaned back. Sylvia Berg?

"How do you know?"

"You see," said Taffy, scrunching her chair around to get closer, "Harry was assisting me in my career." She looked at me and did not blink. "I used to work at his club, and he helped me out. With dance and voice lessons. And sometimes part of the rent."

I was beginning to get the picture.

"Uh-huh," I said. She gave me a look.

"What do you mean by that?" she demanded quietly.

"Nothing."

"All right. So it was all of the rent! A guy like Harry, I earned it!"

"Go on."

"Well, when she found out about me, that was it! She went after Harry and shot him!"

My head was starting to spin, trying to follow the convolutions of Taffy Taliferro.

"Taffy, wait a minute. How do you know Sylvia shot him?"

"I just told you. She found out about us."

"But even so . . . why should she shoot him in that apartment downtown?"

"I don't know why! Ask her! Give her the third degree! Take a rubber hose to her!" Taffy's pert little All-American cheerleader face did not lose its freshness as these sentiments poured out.

"I think something's missing here," I said. "Things aren't adding up."

Well, I was the dumbest newspaper reporter Sally had ever come across, that was clear. Here she was risking her life and her career telling things that the entire New York City Police Department was trying to find out, and there I sat like a fireplug.

"Don't you see?" she said in exasperation. "When Sylvia heard about the fifty thousand dollars she went totally wacko!"

I'm sorry to tell you that I managed to put a Tiparillo cigar into my mouth backward, getting a mouth full of fire and ashes, and jerking it away as though stung by an asp. Taffy's little revelation and the lighted cigar tip had about the same effect on me.

"*You* got the fifty thousand?" I managed to say, licking my blistered lip and experiencing a burning sensation on the tip of my tongue.

"Me? No, no! But that's what Sylvia thinks! Harry gave it to that man, of course. When Sylvia heard about it, she just plain blew up."

"Wait a minute, Taffy. Harry gave some man fifty thousand?"

"Well, yes, of course! How do you think I got out from under the blanket?"

"Blanket?"

"In the car!"

I sipped my Schaefer and relighted my Tiparillo, making sure I put the right end into my mouth. Sally was not only a tap-dancing whiz, she was about as nimble a talker as I'd ever met. I was already feeling devastated that I'd agreed to be her "confidence man," but there was no way to go now but forward.

"Sally," I said, "listen, I think there are some things you haven't told me. Why don't you start at the beginning."

"You mean Kansas City?"

"No. Harry Berg."

"I used to work at the Zebra Club, and . . ."

"Let's skip to Harry giving the man fifty thousand dollars. What's that all about?"

"That's how much he had to pay in ransom! But Sylvia doesn't believe it. She thinks he gave it to me."

I looked at Taffy in bewilderment. "Ransom?"

"Yes, of course, ransom," she said excitedly. "When that man kidnapped me!"

16

I WAS BEGINNING TO realize what it would be like to agree to a story in confidence and then be told who Deep Throat is. Taffy Taliferro, once swearing me to silence, kept pouring out one mad revelation after another. Sylvia Berg had killed her husband, but I couldn't mention that. Taffy herself had been kidnapped and ransomed for $50,000, but I couldn't mention that either. If held back, those two little sputtering bombs alone would engender rage in the excitable natures of Ironhead Matthews and Detective Lawler when they found out.

"Taffy," I said. "I'm not quite clear on what you're trying to tell me."

"You don't seem to know anything," she said in exasperation. "Are you sure you're a reporter?"

"You assume I know more than I do," I said apologetically.

Sally explained that she had waited tables at the Zebra Club while waiting for her show-business break. Harry Berg had noticed her, which was extremely easy to do, and started "assisting her career." Eventually, Sylvia Berg noticed Harry noticing Sally. Suddenly Sally's job was eliminated at the Zebra Club. She hung on, though, and eventually landed a spot in the chorus line of *42nd Street*.

"Everything was wonderful." She sighed. "I was in a show

and Harry was paying the rent. I need help, you know, because I have to have my hair done a lot."

"Oh," I said.

Life was a frothy, bubbling round of dance and voice lessons in the morning, Harry and then the hairdresser in the afternoons, and *42nd Street* at night.

"I really had arrived," she said. "It was so terrific. Everybody in Kansas City hated me. And it had taken only three years!"

And then it had happened.

"I got out of the taxi in my leotards and leg warmers and was just going in for dance lessons when this man grabbed me right on the street and threw me into a car," she said, her voice rising in anger.

"Where was this?"

"Right in front of Jack LaLanne's on Fifty-fifth Street!"

The man was wearing a ski mask over his face so she couldn't recognize him, she went on.

"He shoved me into the backseat of this big black limousine, and threw a blanket over me," she said.

"A blanket?"

"Yes! It was smelly and greasy and sticky, and I thought I would throw up! He put something against me through the blanket and said it was a gun and he would shoot if I didn't keep quiet."

"Then what?"

"Then the car started moving."

Covered with a blanket on the floor behind the front seat, Sally cowered silently in terror as the car moved through traffic. The driver continually reached back over the seat to stick the gun against her, she said.

"I was scared out of my wits."

Finally, she said, the car stopped. Then she heard the man talking on the telephone.

"He got out and went to a phone booth?"

"No. He was still in the car. The phone was in the car. He called up Harry at the Zebra Club."

"While you were still in the car?"

"Yes. He called and got Harry on the phone, and he told him he was holding me. He told Harry to get ready to hand over fifty thousand in cash to a man who would walk in the door at any minute. He told him to put the money in a bag and cover it up with bottles of wine and ice."

"He said a man would walk into the Zebra Club at any minute?"

"Yes!"

"He didn't mean himself?"

"I don't know what he meant. I was under that stupid blanket sick as a cat," she protested. "He told Harry not to ask any questions of the man who came in, but to just hand over the money. Or else!"

"Yeah . . . and then?"

"Then he stuck the phone under the blanket and told me to say Harry's name and nothing else. I could hardly speak, but I finally did. Harry yelled out my name, and then the man pulled the phone away."

"Okay. Then what?"

"That was all!"

"What do you mean 'all'?"

"I stayed under the blanket waiting and listening for about a million years, but the man didn't say anything else. I heard a car drive away. Finally I peeked out and he was gone! I was in the car all by myself. I jumped out and ran like a maniac."

"That was it?"

"Yes."

Loose ends whirled inside my brain.

"Where were you when you got out of the car?"

"Way over on the West Side by the river by the Greyhound Bus Station!"

"What did you do?"

"I ran into a bar and called Harry right away. He came and got me, and I was shaking so, I couldn't talk for five minutes."

"So you don't know what happened to the guy in the ski mask?"

"No."

"What about the limousine?"

"Harry drove me back over by the river and I pointed it out to him. It was still there. I don't know what he did about it."

Harry Berg had told her to say nothing about the incident, she said. He would take care of everything.

"He told me if I said anything, he'd be very mad. And when Harry got very mad, you know, things were likely to be broken. Even parts of people. He said it would ruin my career if anything got out about it. I think he meant it would ruin him if his wife found out about it. So I promised, and Harry gave me some jade earrings."

"You never told the police?"

"Harry told me not to! I told nobody! I thought it was all over. But then Sylvia came after me and said I'd better give her back that money. I said I didn't know anything about it, and she stuck a gun in my face and said she'd empty it into my head! I closed my eyes and screamed until she left. Then she went out and shot Harry!"

She took a breath, rolled her eyes around, and went on.

"What am I going to do? If that money hasn't turned up yet, Sylvia will be back! If the police find out, I'll be written up in the *National Enquirer* and kicked out of the show and everybody in Kansas City will die laughing. You've got to help me."

"How?"

"Tell the police Sylvia shot Harry and that man in the ski mask got the money. But don't mention me."

Was that all?

"Where did the money come from, anyway?" I asked.

"From Harry's gambling clubs."

"How many did he have?"

"I don't know. Two or three. I worked in two of them. He always counted the money in his office in the Zebra Club in the morning."

"Do you know a comic named Trigger Moran?"

Taffy made a face. "Oh, sure. He worked for Harry too."

"Doing what?"

Taffy's eyes narrowed. "All he ever did as far as I'm concerned is bump into me every chance he got."

I looked at the petite stick of dynamite and tried to figure out what to do. Finding out who Deep Throat is would be easier.

"What about the man who threw you into the car? What was he like?"

"A dirty son-of-a-bitch!"

"Yes, but what did he look like?"

"Like a skier."

"A what?"

"He had a ski mask on."

"Well, was he tall or short, fat or thin, old or young?"

Taffy pondered that, frowning and trying to bring back the image. "Sort of medium all around."

"Could he have been about forty-eight?"

"Oh, no. Younger. He was strong."

"Could it have been Trigger Moran?"

"Well, I don't know! He had on that mask, and I was afraid to look at him anyway."

"What was his voice like?"

"He had a funny accent. Like that old-time movie star."

"Humphrey Bogart?"

Taffy beamed. "You do know something! Yes, Humphrey Bogart. So now that you know who he is, can you get him arrested without mentioning me?"

"I don't know who he is," I said. "When did all this happen?"

"About three weeks ago."

"Do you know what day it was?"

"Oh, yes. Friday. I go to dance lessons Monday, Wednesday and Friday."

"About what time?"

"It was just before nine. The class starts at nine, and I was just going in."

A man in a ski mask—our old pal Humphrey Bogart, evidently—kidnapped Taffy in a car and drove her to the river. He called Harry Berg and said a man would walk in in a few minutes to pick up $50,000 ransom. That had to have been Howard Ritter. Ritter put the money into a red bag and walked to the excursion boat, where he went on board. Taffy sat up and realized Ski Mask was gone. It seemed logical to believe that Ski Mask had gone on board the boat with Ritter. Then somebody shot Ritter on the boat, and the red bag went over the stern.

The kidnapper certainly knew a lot about Harry Berg. He knew about Taffy. He knew Harry counted gambling money in the morning. He knew Harry would not go to the cops about it.

It was wonderful that Taffy had given me all this arcane information. All it led to were twice as many new questions.

Harry Berg had clearly discovered that the man who picked up the ransom was Howard Ritter, and had gone to Ritter's apartment to get his money back. I could answer that question anyway. Howard Ritter's picture and the story of his murder on the riverboat had been in the *Daily Press* the next day, along with his address. Berg hadn't gone there to see Jennifer.

That brought me to another lovely question. Who had shot Harry Berg at Jennifer's apartment? And why? If it were the same guy we saw, the one who fired a shot at me, it ruled out Sylvia.

"Well?" said Sally Taliferro, bringing me back to Broadway Joe's and the mural of famous faces. "What are you going to do?"

"I wish I knew," I said. "We have to find that guy in the ski mask."

"But didn't you hear what I said about Sylvia Berg?"

"Sylvia couldn't have shot Harry," I said.

"I'm telling you," insisted Taffy, getting up. "You'd better listen to me."

I walked Taffy outside and over to Eighth Avenue, where she hailed a cab and went rolling uptown, apparently feeling a lot better now that she had shifted her burdens onto me. I didn't feel so hot, though. Every time a reporter takes a story in confidence, he swears he'll never do it again. I certainly won't!

17

I REMEMBER PROFESSOR WELCH at the University of
Missouri describing the worst predicament possible as "being
in Fort Sumter." It was a Union fort sitting out in the middle
of the harbor of Charleston, South Carolina, and when the
Civil War started, the garrison found itself surrounded on all
sides by six batteries of Confederate brass cannon on the
shores. The sixty-eight Union soldiers inside were ordered not
to surrender, and didn't dare open fire. When you were in
Fort Sumter you were in a fix, and when I walked into the
Daily Press city room the next day, it was obvious I'd gone
through a time warp and that it was 1861 and I was in
Charleston harbor looking down the muzzles of General
Beauregard's artillery. Except that General Beauregard closely
resembled Ironhead Matthews.

"What the hell do you mean you got the story in confidence?" he complained.

"She wouldn't talk otherwise."

"Can't you even outwit a goddamn tap-dancer?" He
chomped on his cigar and glared at me. "So what did the
little twit have to say?"

I tried to relate Taffy's adventures, but it was hard to talk
over Ironhead's crazed interruptions. "What?" he shouted.
"This story had a kidnap and a ransom in it?"

"That's what Taffy said."

"Berg paid fifty grand to get her free? She must be some firecracker."

"She is," I admitted.

Ironhead gave me a look that can only be described as sneering. "But we can't run her picture or her name because she was too smart for our reporter."

I stood there like a kid facing the school principal.

"Okay," Ironhead muttered. "Write what you can. Make it sing, and for God's sake, try to make sense." I was in Fort Sumter, all right.

When I got to my desk, the phone was ringing. It was Theresa at the reception desk, and she said a Max Kasian was waiting to see me. I still didn't know who he was. I walked out of the city room, down the hall past sports and to the reception desk.

A dapper, suntanned man popped to his feet as soon as he saw me, and took two quick steps forward. "Mr. Fitzgerald?"

"Yes."

"Max Kasian," he said smiling disarmingly. "Columbia National Insurance Company." He wore a gray striped summer suit and a bow tie.

I tried to figure out the reason for his visit, but nothing occured to me.

"What can I do for you?"

Max Kasian stepped closer and adopted a confidential tone of voice and manner, as though he and I were partners in some undercover venture. "Lawler told me you were on the Ritter story. We insured Howard Ritter."

"Oh," I said. I remembered vaguely that Jennifer had found an insurance policy in her father's papers.

"Something irregular about it," said Max Kasian. "There's always something irregular when it's double indemnity."

"What was double indemnity?"

"Ritter's death benefit for his daughter. It was double for accidental death while traveling. Doesn't that sound funny to you?"

I looked at him. He watched me expectantly, as though my approval meant everything.

"I don't know," I said. "I don't think she even knew anything about the policy."

Max Kasian turned his face sideways and glanced at me as though I were surely kidding him. "Oh, she knew, all right," he smiled. "She knew."

I looked at Kasian and frowned. He seemed to be talking to me from around a corner, peeking out.

"I just wondered if you could fill me in," he went on. "If you want to use a story that we're not paying the claim, you can. But you didn't get it from us."

Mr. Suntan was beginning to annoy me. Insurance companies are wonderful about dunning people to pay their premiums but not so wonderful about paying claims.

"Why aren't you paying it?" I asked.

Max Kasian smiled knowingly. "If the deceased were involved in criminal activity, we're off the hook."

"By criminal activity, you mean getting killed?"

"We have reason to believe he was mixed up in something," he smiled. "That's what the police tell us."

"Um-hmmm," I said. "What do you want from me?"

"Well, you've been covering the story. You might know a lot more than we do. Maybe you could fill us in on what you've come up with. We'll pay for it, of course."

"Anything I know is in the paper."

"Yes, but there are lots of other things you must have picked up that might help us disprove this claim."

I took two steps away from him and then stopped and looked back. "Get out of here," I managed, although I was shaking so much, I almost let him have it.

He looked surprised. "What?"

"Go fuck yourself," I said, and walked down the hall and back into the city room. The goddamn slimy worm in his summer suit. I didn't like him or his company. I was getting sick and tired of the whole story. But that didn't make it go away.

115

Part of my trouble, of course, was that I was carrying around dynamite and needed a place to put it down.

I called Big Jim Lawler and filled him in on the kidnap story so it wouldn't come as a surprise when he saw it in the paper. Cops hate to read things in the paper that they don't know. They hate it even worse if their lieutenant reads it.

I got an even less enthusiastic reception from Lawler. "Goddamn it," he yelled, "don't start complicating a two-bit gambling murder."

"Lawless, I'm telling you there's more to this than I thought. Harry's girlfriend was kidnapped and Harry paid fifty grand in ransom to get her loose."

There was a silence. I could imagine Jim Lawler shaking his head in disgust. "Now, who told you that?"

"See, that's just it. I can't tell you. But it's true. A guy wearing a ski mask snatched Harry's girl, and got fifty thousand out of him. It looks like Howard Ritter picked up the ransom."

"Goddamn it, that was a gambling debt," he snapped. "I don't want to hear about ransoms."

I explained that the only reason I was telling him even this much was because the guy the Police Department wanted was the guy in the ski mask.

"Is that the one who killed Berg?" he wanted to know.

"You got me."

"Who's Harry's girlfriend that got snatched?"

"I can't tell you that, Lawless."

"Who do you think you are, Fitz, a privileged character? You can't tell me and you expect me to take this seriously?"

"I got it in confidence."

"There's nothing confidential in a murder case, you goddamn idiot!"

Well, Lawless pumped me and yelled and threatened, but I had to tell him that everything I was able to say would be in the *Daily Press*. I also filled him in on Trigger Moran, and suggested he ask the little comic some questions.

"I already did," Lawler came back.

116

"You did?"

"Yes! We're not sitting here watching soap operas! He's got an alibi for the Harry Berg thing. You. And he says he was home asleep when Ritter got it."

"Asleep, huh?"

"That's what he says. And I can't prove otherwise."

"How about the Bogart imitation on the tape?"

"He denies it's him. He said the same words for us into a tape and we did a voice print on him. It's not him. Anyway, we couldn't hold him."

"Wonderful."

"You're welcome."

I wrote the story as best I could, giving the mysterious Ski Mask the most attention. But there was also the "unidentified Broadway show girl" who had been kidnapped by Ski Mask and ransomed by Harry Berg. There was also the "allegation" that Howard Ritter had picked up the ransom money just before he was murdered.

It was a pretty good story, and finally Jennifer had her wish. Her father's picture was printed: as bagman in a kidnap-ransom that had left two people dead.

When I got home to East Eighty-second Street that evening, I filled Jennifer in so she wouldn't be too shocked when the three-star edition came out.

"Oh, boy," she said softly.

"I'm sorry."

"It's not your fault."

She understood that I had to follow the story wherever it led, and if that were the story, then she realized I had to print it. That's what she said. But behind her words was something else.

"There was nothing else you could do," she said resignedly, which I translated as, "You're dragging me and my father deeper and deeper into this."

"I'm really sorry," I mumbled.

"It's all right." It sounded to me like "Goodbye."

That was about the time things began to unravel between us. I couldn't blame her. But the only direction open to me was to follow my nose. It got even worse. Stories came out linking Jenny to Harry Berg. That came from Sylvia. I knew it was nonsense, but that didn't keep it from hurting.

Jennifer fell into a sort of numbed melancholia. Being battered by that great anonymous monster The Media can bring it on. The more I tried to help Jenny by digging into the case, the worse it got.

"Who is doing this?" she would ask me, her deep brown eyes looking helpless.

"I wish I knew." I spared her my endless ticktacktoe game. "It hasn't come together yet."

"I'm beginning to hope it never does." She sighed.

We might have weathered those choppy seas if it hadn't been for the phone call one night. Jennifer was closest to the phone and she answered it.

"Hello?" Jennifer said. She paused, turning around, trying to hear better. "What? Yes . . . he's right here . . . what? Jennifer. Jennifer Ritter. Who's this?"

I had looked up from my book, sensing something sticky developing. Jennifer stared at me quizzically and then she held out the phone.

"It's somebody named Belinda."

I hurried to the phone. It was Belinda Sharpe from Wales, and the first thing she asked was, "Who is that woman?"

I tried to explain logically who Jennifer was and, more to the point, what she was doing at East Eight-second Street. The distance between New York and Wales kept increasing with each lame sentence. By the end of the conversation, I knew I could stop waiting for Belinda to return.

When I hung up and looked at Jennifer, I realized I had troubles a lot closer than Wales.

"I think it's safe for me to move back home," she said.

18

THE NEXT DAY WE loaded her things into the Falcon and I drove her back downtown to Gramercy Park. Naturally, it was raining, and we both got drenched carrying her things from my apartment to the car and again from the car to her building on Irving Place.

We sat in her apartment smoking, darting glances at each other and then looking away. It was over, that was clear, but we went through the meaningless polite ritual of talking vacantly about the rain. There was a phone call, and that helped break up the tension for a minute, but it was a wrong number.

"Well . . ." I said, and stood up.

"Yes."

"I'll let you know if I hear anything from Lawler."

"Sure. Thanks."

I took a tentative step toward her, and she got up and gave me a perfunctory kiss. I smiled, and walked outside to the Falcon. It had stopped raining, but that didn't help much.

During the next couple of days I checked with Lawler and Santelli a few times, but they had nothing to report. No new leads or witnesses had surfaced. The Howard Ritter case slid deeper into their homicide file as newer and more urgent murders occupied their time. The case had reached a too-typical resolution; unsolved and as good as forgotten.

I sat in Costello's after work, staring at my face in the mirror. I didn't look so terrific. I looked like a person with a toothache. I knew what it was, all right.

I had stuck my nose into things and stirred them up and hung out Howard Ritter to dry as a bagman in a kidnapping. It mightn't have been so bad if Jennifer had railed and screamed at me. But that silence, that defeated, whimpering retreat back down to Gramercy Park—that tormented me. The thing is, I knew nothing more would happen in the case unless there was a break, more or less by accident. Nobody much cared about the case except Jennifer. And the only person she had to depend upon to help was a traitor who kept stomping on her fingers when she tried to pull herself out of the water.

That's who I saw looking back out at me in Costello's. And I guess that's why I found myself over on the West Side at the Hudson River gazing at the riverboat one morning.

Howard Ritter had walked into the Zebra Club and had come out with $50,000 ransom in a bag topped off with wine and ice. He had walked to the cruise line and gotten aboard. What then? Who had met him aboard and shot him?

Taffy had told me she was in a rented limousine "way over by the river" when Ski Mask disappeared. She had heard a car drive away, and had seen a Greyhound Bus sign. That had confused me, because that seemed to indicate the Port Authority Bus Terminal on Eighth Avenue, which is four blocks from the river. But as I walked around in front of the riverboat pier, I saw it. Right across Twelfth Avenue was a big sign on a building: GREYHOUND PACKAGE EXPRESS ENTRANCE. That could have been what Taffy saw. I walked over and stood under it on Twelfth Avenue at Fortieth Street. From there I had a clear view of the excursion boat across the avenue. If Ski Mask had been parked there in his rented limousine, he could have watched Ritter go on board the boat with his package. Taffy had heard a car drive off, but that couldn't have been Ski Mask. He must have gone aboard the boat after Ritter and killed him. What had happened? Had they quarreled over the money? That would mean Ritter was in on it. I realized I was still clinging to the hope that somehow he wasn't. Maybe as far as he was concerned, he was delivering cold wine to the eccentric Mr. Goodman on the boat.

As all this spun in my head, I was walking toward the excursion boat. A young man wearing a blue blazer was talking to me and I realized I was at the gangplank.

"Ticket?"

I went back to the ticket window and got a ticket to Bear Mountain, the first stop, and walked aboard the boat to have a quick look around. I could check out the stern and the top deck and hop off before it pulled out.

All around me, people were streaming aboard carrying picnic baskets, blankets, paper bags, hampers, plastic bags. No one would have thought anything about Ritter's red bag. The picnickers spread out on the four decks of the excursion boat, setting up tables and chairs singly and in rows around the decks along the railings. For thousands of tenement-dwelling New Yorkers, it was Big Apple air conditioning, a breezy nine-hour vacation up the Hudson River to Bear Mountain, Hyde Park, and back. Most got off at Bear Mountain, had a picnic, and then caught the boat back in the afternoon.

We had found Ritter's body on the main deck at the back in the cafeteria section. It was enclosed by windows that ran all the way around the curve of the stern. There were Formica-topped tables in the center, and booths around the sides and stern. One booth was directly in the curve at the very back, and that's where Ritter had been sitting.

I walked back to the booth and sat down. The windows were only a few inches above the table of the booth, and they slid open sideways easily. I looked out. The water was only a few feet below. This had to have been where the red bag went overboard.

I inspected the rest of the boat. There's an open deck right over the cafeteria. You could look down over the stern from there, but you couldn't look into the cafeteria. That was where Stu Kravitz and Eva Stegman had been.

The two upper decks were set forward of the stern, and from there you couldn't see anything over the back. I looked across at the Greyhound Package Express sign and could see it clearly. It seemed odd at first that it was moving, since it's on the side of a warehouse. And then I realized it wasn't the building that was moving.

When I got to the tiny purser's office on the main deck a few minutes later, I found out that I could not make a ship-to-shore phone call unless it was life or death.

"It is," I said through the vertical bars of the purser's office. "Ironhead will kill me!"

The youthful purser asked me to explain, but I realized it was hopeless. "When do we get to Bear Mountain?"

"Twelve-thirty," he said cheerfully, not caring that by then, I would be back in Fort Sumter again.

I straggled back into the stern cafeteria and got bacon and eggs with hash browns and some coffee. I took a booth to the side and thought sourly of my probable short future at the *Daily Press*. The boat pulled out at seven minutes after ten, and went pounding briskly up the river.

I sat there over my breakfast, staring at the stern and wondering why the red bag had gone overboard. Somebody certainly knew there was more than wine in the bag. But why throw it over the stern? Or had Ritter dropped it over the side when he was shot?

Out the window on the Manhattan side, I saw a cluster of boats in a marina. The Seventy-ninth Street Boat Basin. A mass of boats of all sizes floated inside the basin's breakwater, and there were a couple of big yachts anchored in the river outside the basin.

As I sat in the cafeteria, I imagined Ritter in the booth at the stern with his bag. Even as I ate, I realized the cafeteria was virtually empty. Even though the prices were modest, the people who rode the riverboat on weekdays apparently either couldn't afford them or preferred their own food and the open decks. They were at picnic tables on the decks eating hard-boiled eggs, watermelon, and fried chicken brought from home. By the time somebody announced over the PA system that we were approaching the George Washington Bridge, the cafeteria was deserted except for me.

It was about ten-thirty when we reached the bridge, which is about where and when Ritter apparently was shot. I had wondered how anyone could be shot on a crowded excursion boat and go unnoticed, but now it was obvious.

On a post in the center of the cafeteria was a sign: PLEASE! NO LOUNGING OR CARD PLAYING IN CAFETERIA AREA. If you wanted to remain, you had to buy something. The cafeteria was the one corner of the boat that was both sheltered and almost empty.

Looking out over the river from the stern, I tried to imagine a cabin cruiser following the riverboat. "It fished the bag out of the water and turned back," Stu Kravitz had said. It had to have been that inflatable "beach" thing that Miss Grady told us about.

Turned back to where? The only destination I could imagine was the Seventy-ninth Street Boat Basin back down the river a few minutes, or a yacht anchored in the river.

Could our mysterious Mr. Goodman have put out from the boat basin that day? Was it possible that he had arranged this rather roundabout way of getting wine delivered to him aboard his yacht? Or was the real cargo the money under the ice?

I walked around to the purser's office and asked how many were aboard and if it was like most weekdays. There were 1,062 on the boat, and yes, it was about average.

"How fast does the boat go upriver?" I asked.

"Sixteen knots," he said.

There was nothing to do except go out on deck and watch the lovely Hudson River Valley glide by. The sun was bright under blue skies and the boat left a foamy wake as it churned

123

upriver. From the open deck over the cafeteria I could see smaller boats darting about the river—cabin cruisers, speedboats, occasional sailboats. You weren't likely to pay much attention to them, or to notice something go over the side.

I strolled back to the purser's office and asked the young blond purser if he remembered the day Ritter was killed.

He looked nervous as he glanced through the cage at me. "No, sir," he said, "I don't know a thing."

Had anyone seen a cruiser following the riverboat, or a bag go over the stern?

"No, sir, I don't know anything about that. As far as I know, nobody knew anything until the body was discovered. I really can't discuss it, sir."

So much for my cunning ways of wheedling information out of people.

I really could have enjoyed the ride up the river, through wooded hills on both sides, if it hadn't been for the fact that I was supposed to be at the *Daily Press*.

As promised, the excursion boat turned around and squealed against a wharf at the Bear Mountain landing at twelve-thirty. From the landing it's a winding, climbing, hairpin-turn trail up the side of the mountain, past the blue-green swimming pool and the log bathhouse that looks as though it had been constructed by the Algonquin Indians. Farther up, the trail levels off among picnic tables along the shore of a lake dotted with aluminum rowboats, and finally there's the Bear Mountain Inn, which I hoped was a repository of telephones. Bear Mountain Inn is all fieldstone walls and timbers, a Swiss chalet with two squat, iron bears that look like Winnie the Pooh on either side of the front door.

I hurried inside, found a pay phone in the gift shop, and called Ironhead. He seemed to have a stubborn preoccupation with time, because the first thing he said was, "Do you know what time it is?" And then he wanted to know where I was.

"Ironhead, listen, you know that ski-mask kidnapper?"

"Who?"

124

"Well, he wasn't in on it alone."

"No, that actor was in on it too."

"Listen, Ironhead, if Ski Mask got Ritter, then that means there was another guy. The guy in the cabin cruiser."

"What cabin cruiser?"

"The one that was following the riverboat and got the bag out of the river. That's the guy we have to find. Unless he was just delivering wine to a yacht in the river."

I could hear Ironhead making choking sounds, and then he must have spat. "Where are you?" he demanded.

"Bear Mountain."

"Bear Mountain?" He started cursing violently. "If you're not in here by one, you're in big trouble."

I looked at my watch. It was five minutes to one. Clearly, a monumental mistake had been made. "But Ironhead . . ."

Bang! Errrrrrrrrrrrrr. Silence.

I walked up the stairs into the mammoth, wood-ceilinged dining room, where there was a huge stone fireplace guarded by two more Winnie the Poohs. In one corner was a grand piano, and in the other a little bar.

I walked over and ordered a Schaefer and asked the bartender how long it would take to get back to Manhattan. He said it would take two hours and $75 to $100 by cab, or I could wait until four-thirty and go back down the river on the boat.

"Any way I could get there by one?" I asked.

"It's ten after one now."

I drank my Schaefer and looked out over the lawn, where there was a flagpole flanked by two old black Revolutionary War cannon.

19

IARRIVED BACK AT Forty-first Street on the riverboat at seven o'clock that night. All I had to show for the day was an underwater, gurgling, goldfish feeling in my head. There was nothing to do at the Bear Mountain Inn except look out at the cannon and have a few Schaefers. Once back on the boat, there was nothing to do riding downriver but to have a few more. By the time I walked down the gangplank, things were coming at me filtered through water and a bubbling air pump. But the message got through anyway—I was deeper than ever inside Ironhead's doghouse.

I sloshed to my green Falcon in the parking lot and drove home, my head swarming with ideas. It occurred to me that Ski Mask must have been aboard the riverboat that day it returned with Howard Ritter's body on the stern, and that meant Big Jim Lawler's movie camera got a picture of him. But unless he still wore the ski mask, how could you pick him out of fourteen hundred people?

I collapsed into bed. By morning, the concrete-slab monster had done his work. The right side of my head was solid rock from behind my eye to the back of my head.

I drove to the *Daily Press* and got an Alka-Seltzer and a

Pepsi at the newsstand in the lobby. Upstairs in the city room, I drank the Alka-Seltzer and the Pepsi and waited for the slag in my head to dissolve.

There was a message at the switchboard to call Lawler, which perked me up a little. But when I reached the squad, the sergeant would only tell me that Lawler had gone to Jennifer's apartment.

"What for?" I asked through the sun spots.

"I don't know. Maybe to have tea," the sergeant muttered.

I hung up and was trying to sort that out when the Apparition appeared before me, its jaws working.

"Well?" said the Apparition.

"Listen, Ironhead," I mumbled, "something may be breaking in the Ritter case."

"Is that why you went to Bear Mountain?"

"No, I mean now. A detective's at Ritter's place."

"Why?"

"I don't know. You want me to go have a look?"

"Since you won't stay off the story, I might as well let you keep it. But goddamn it, I don't want to get a call that you're in Butte, Montana!"

"Okay."

Ironhead studied my painfully hung-over face, and his jaws worked. "I'd really like to know what the hell you were doing at Bear Mountain," he said, "but I haven't got time to listen to one of your explanations."

"Well, see . . ."

"Never mind.".

". . . Ski Mask must have been on the boat . . ."

"Get the hell out of here!"

I left. When I got to Jennifer's apartment, there was a uniformed cop on the door, and Detective Lawler was inside.

"What's going on?" I asked, stepping in.

Lawler mumbled something and looked away, nodding his head toward somebody standing by the fireplace. I glanced that way. Jennifer was sitting on the couch, about ready to

128

detonate, and beside her, standing stiffly with his briefcase in both hands in front of him, was Max Kasian, the suntanned investigator for Columbia National Insurance.

"They want the place searched," Lawler said with a show of annoyance.

"Who?"

He nodded at the dapper Max. "Insurance company. They got a court order. They think the fifty thousand is here someplace." He lit a cigarette. "Actually, I'd rather find the gun."

"What gun?" I asked, getting perturbed.

"Any gun, Fitz. Any gun." He walked over to where Santelli was digging through papers in a desk. I took a few steps toward Jennifer, who looked disgusted.

"Hi," I said.

"Hello," she said grimly.

Max Kasian still wore that self-satisfied expression suggesting that he possessed vast stores of inside information.

"What are you looking for?" I challenged.

"What do you think?" he smiled knowingly.

Jennifer was boiling. "He thinks I've got the money," she told me. "I think he wants me arrested. He thinks Daddy was in on the whole thing."

Max Kasian's expression got even more haughty. "Listen to this," he smirked. "You expect us to pay a claim like this? The man is involved in a felony and gets killed? Besides, riding an excursion boat is not, strictly speaking, traveling."

"What is it?" Jennifer demanded.

"Joyriding! He wasn't going anywhere. Just up the river and back. That's not traveling."

"My father was terrified of flying, but he had to fly when he got work," Jennifer explained.

"So, you admit he wasn't traveling to a job," Max pounced triumphantly.

"Listen, you creep," Jennifer shot back, rising to face him. "I didn't even know about this policy, but now I'm getting every last penny out of you! You got that?"

129

Santelli walked over to Lawler and they stood there in the center of the room, shaking their heads and gesturing.

Lawler sighed. "Mr. Kasian, we can't find any money or any guns. You want to look, be my guest."

"Touch one thing and see what happens," Jennifer declared.

"She squirreled it away somewhere," Max yelled, his voice rising ten feet. "This claim is being held up until things are clarified," he went on pompously. He grabbed his fat, brown briefcase and stalked furiously out of the apartment.

"Sorry," said Lawler, turning to leave also. We exchanged glances and he looked away. I knew perfectly well that the apartment could not have been searched unless Lawler wanted it searched, no matter what any insurance company said. He didn't tell that to Jennifer, and neither did I. At least, though, Jennifer was finally in the clear.

"We found your dancer friend Sally," he said.

"I thought you would," I said, relieved that I had not blown the whistle on her. "What did she tell you?"

"The same thing she told you," he came back.

"What do you make of it all?"

Lawler shook his head. "I don't know. But it looks like Ritter and the guy in the ski mask were in it together. Which would be enough to shoot down that insurance policy."

I didn't like the way Lawler's mind was working. When a case drags on and no good suspects can be located, the person closest to the crime slips more and more into jeopardy. I didn't tell Jennifer that either.

After they left, Jennifer sank down onto the couch, looking destroyed. We sat there in a stupor, not talking.

She put her face between her hands and her elbows on her knees and stared straight ahead.

"I want you to drop the case," she said flatly.

"What?"

"I can't take any more," she went on, her voice trembly. "The police think my father's in on it. That disgusting insurance man thinks so." She glanced at me. "You even think so."

"Well . . ."

"Never mind. Drop it." She covered her face. "Because if this keeps up, maybe I'll even start believing it."

I lighted a Tiparillo. How could I tell her that I couldn't drop it now? It's very difficult to get the press interested in a murder story, but once we get our teeth into it, we see it through to the bitter end.

"Give me one of those," she said.

I unwrapped one of the slim cigars for her, and realized I was out of matches. She dug into a mass of discarded papers and matchbooks on the coffee table and picked out a book of matches. I took them and lighted her cigar. She puffed and gazed at the book of matches and kept staring. Then she reached over and took them out of my hand. The cover was bright gold and across the front in black was a single word, MULLIGAN'S.

"Where did these come from?" she asked, her mind zeroing in tighter and tighter on the book of matches.

"You just pulled them from that pile of papers," I said. "Why?"

She stared a hole into the matchbook. "I lighted a Tiparillo with these matches the night we found . . . him on the floor. Didn't I?"

"I don't know."

"I did! I remember now. Where did they come from? I've never been to any Mulligan's. She looked at me, her eyes wide. "Fitz, that man must have dropped them."

"Harry Berg?"

"No. The other one! The one that shot Berg. He was sitting here on the couch waiting, Lawler said, smoking. When Berg came in, he shot him. Whoever he was, he must have left these matches."

Her hand trembled as she looked at them.

"I must have picked them up without thinking about it."

131

I opened the matchbook. Inside was the address of Mulligan's, on West Forty-seventh Street.

"We have to go and see," she said, and hope was back in her lovely face again. It was all right with me. I had nothing else to do.

When we drove over to the place that night, we found a nightclub with a large sign, MULLIGAN'S, in black and gold across the front. Inside there was a long, cozy bar with a fireplace in one wall. Beyond the bar was a back room with a little stage. We slid onto barstools and looked around in the gloom. When the bartender stepped over, we got another surprise. It was Angelo Pinzino's friend Barney Wells, the former emcee from Going Up.

"Well," he said. "Hello."

I asked one of those brilliant questions. "You work here?"

"I fill in sometimes," he said. "What'll it be?"

We ordered, and when he brought the white wine and Schaefer he stood there watching us pensively. "Is there a show in the back?" I finally asked.

"Yeah, they got a show. I did my act here once."

"You did?"

"Yeah, I did. I've worked lots of places." He apparently wanted to impress us that he was somebody.

"How's the boat thing coming?" I asked conversationally.

"Good," he smiled smugly. "It's in the bag."

"Who owns this place?" Jennifer interrupted.

"Sutty Larson," said Barney. "Why?"

"Where can we find him?" I asked.

Barney nodded toward the back room. "In the back, usually."

Jennifer and I took our drinks and walked into the back entertainment room to a table. A waitress brought us menus about a yard high, which we looked at with little interest. Suddenly nails dug into my hand. Jennifer was squeezing me frantically. I looked, and she was staring wide-eyed over the top of her immense menu.

I shot a look across the room, following her glance. A large, beefy man in a blue shirt and a blue suit was standing by the wall, his fleshy face set in a fixed expression of challenge and intimidation. His large, flat eyes were rigidly locked upon us.

Jennifer didn't have to tell me. It was the "other man" who had come to her apartment. She darted a look at me and her eyes left no doubt about it. We had gone looking for the killer of Harry Berg, and he had found us.

20

ASHADOWY FORM LOOMED up in front of us about then and with an "Ulp!" Jennifer swallowed five pounds of air. The waitress was as startled by her reaction as Jennifer was by the appearance of the waitress.

"What do you want!" Jennifer blurted out, which added to the waitress's confusion.

"Huh?"

Jennifer appealed to me, her face flushed and her eyes like billiard balls. "What are we going to do?" she whispered.

The waitress leaned closer, trying to hear. "You want to order now?"

"Order?" said Jennifer.

The waitress put her green order pad into her uniform pocket. "I'll be back," she huffed.

I looked across the room for the Cro-Magnon in blue. He wasn't there anymore. "Are you sure that's the guy?"

Jennifer nodded emphatically, her eyes still wide. She apparently couldn't speak. I figured the man in blue either had gone to the front of Mulligan's so he could watch us when we left, or to get some reinforcements to come and deal with us. Either way, it was time for us to get out of there while we still could.

I signaled the waitress. "Where's the men's room?" I asked her softly.

"In front by the bar," she said.

"Damn," I muttered. "How about the ladies' room?"

She gave me a slantwise look, and then eyed Jennifer. "Over there," she said, jerking her head toward the rear beside the little stage.

"Thanks," I said.

She watched us. "You want to order?"

"Bring us a drink," I said, wanting to send her into the front bar area, out of sight.

She looked at the table. The Schaefer and white wine we had carried in from the bar sat before us. "Another one?"

"Yeah," I replied.

She rolled her eyes, shrugged as if to say she was only the waitress, and walked away.

"Come on," I told Jennifer, getting up and dragging her across past the stage to the ladies' room. She was holding my hand, stumbling along behind me. When we got into the small hallway where the ladies' room was, I saw what I had hoped to find: an exit door. I shoved down the metal bar that opened the door and we plunged out into a narrow, dark alley beside the club. I dragged Jenny protestingly past garbage cans and empty cardboard wine boxes and an overflowing metal garbage bin toward Forty-seventh Street. Behind us I heard a crash and a curse and a shout. Somebody else was coming through the alley.

We came skittering out onto Forty-seventh Street, and Jennifer managed to get on the other side of a couple who were walking by. The man wore a straw hat and the woman looked like she was from Ohio. She was talking about Mamma Leone's when we caught them between us.

"Eddie," Jennifer cried, and I tried to drag her around the couple, but they apparently thought we were muggers and started yelling.

"Shut up, goddamn it," I shouted at them, which didn't calm them down any.

"Let go," I told Jennifer frantically. By now we were all

136

wrapped around each other and wedged between two parked cars.

"Don't get excited," the man said to me, adopting a tone one might use when trying to calm a runaway horse. "My wallet's in my breast pocket."

"I don't want your damned wallet!" I raged at him.

"Oh, my God, Harold, he wants me!" the woman shrieked.

I finally wriggled my hand out of Jennifer's death grip, got past them, and grabbed her hand again. We ran dementedly across the street and half a block west to my car. I could hear footsteps behind us and somebody shouting.

It took at least a year to get the Falcon door open. I pushed Jennifer into the front seat ahead of me in a tumble of arms and legs, and shoved in after her, sprawling across her. I got the door locked just as a great, muscular gorilla's paw clamped on the door handle and tried to pull it open.

I ignored both Jennifer's shrill complaints that I was sitting on her and the savage raging of King Kong on the other side of the car door. Finally the car started. At the same time the side window shattered into a spider web of cracks and mashed pulp. King Kong had tried to put his ham fist through it and almost succeeded.

The Falcon lurched forward. *Clump!* I hit the car parked in front of me.

"Ahhhhhhhhrrgh!" howled King Kong and put his knee into the door. He was also reaching into his jacket for what I imagined was a .38.

I shoved the gearshift into reverse, hurtling backward into another parked car, and then leaped forward out of the parking place. Off we went, lurching down the street followed by the howling maniac. At Ninth Avenue I saw through the rearview mirror that King Kong was no longer behind us. Then the damned cougher gasped and died.

"Don't stop!" Jennifer shrieked, finally getting out from under me. "What are you doing?"

I turned the ignition key frantically. The engine groaned

and sputtered. My foot almost went through the floorboard as I stomped on the gas. "My God, I've flooded it!" I muttered. Then the car started, and off we went. But by then, two headlights were behind us.

I headed south down Ninth Avenue and just made a green light at Forty-fifth Street. When I looked into the rearview mirror, I saw the big black car behind me had run the red light and was gaining fast. Why had I not gotten a real car? I wondered miserably. In my '69 Falcon with only four of the six cylinders hitting, I couldn't outrun an oxcart.

"I can't lose him," I said.

"Go faster!" Jennifer screeched.

But the Falcon's idea of going faster was a moaning, lumbering sputter. I managed to keep on the other side of a truck and then a taxi as we went south across Forty-second Street, but there was no way I could get away from the blue suited Ostrogoth. Going through the Thirties, the black car drew abreast—it was an immense, arrogant Lincoln—and sideswiped us, sending the Falcon into a wobbling swerve that almost put us into the back of the General Post Office.

I can't tell you from what depths of terror a possible glimmer of hope sprang, but suddenly I saw a slim chance. Ahead was West Twentieth Street. By the time we got to it, the M-60 tank was alongside us again, trying once more to sideswipe us. I swung a sharp left onto West Twentieth, causing King Kong to hit his brakes with a screech. He had to back up to follow us. We coughed and sputtered across to Eighth Avenue, where a goddamn red light caught us.

"Run it!" Jennifer shouted.

I edged out into the avenue, but then the light turned green, and the Falcon limped across with the Lincoln once more gaining on us. Halfway up the block I told Jennifer, "Get on the floor!"

"What?"

"I'm going to stop!"

"You're going to *what*?"

138

"Hold on!"

I hit the brakes, which were about the only things on the gasper that really worked well. The Falcon groaned, swayed, and shuddered to a halt in the middle of West Twentieth Street, which is one-way, narrow, and clogged with cars parked on both sides. Jennifer hit the floor, holding her head with both arms and yelling something. I threw the Falcon into reverse and hit the gas pedal. Jennifer let out a howl of fright.

I heard the Lincoln's tires squeal as King Kong tried frantically to stop on the crowded side street. The onrushing Lincoln and my backward-going Falcon met with a stupendous crunch, followed by broken glass and the tinkling of chrome snapping off and rolling across the street. The Falcon slammed into the Lincoln like a Spaldeen against a tenement stoop and rebounded forward into a parked blue-and-white police cruiser. Then the Lincoln wedged itself against the Falcon and burrowed into the side of another police car. We were right in front of the Tenth Precinct station house, and through the dust and the ache in my head and neck I surmised we had totaled at least three blue and white New York City police cars.

"Are you all right?" I asked Jennifer, who was a screaming, doubled-up ball on the floor under the dashboard. She yelled like a Kamikaze pilot and tried to kick me.

I tried to open the door, but it was bent like the corrugated roof of a chicken shed. I heard lots of yelling, and lights were flashing, and somebody yanked open the door.

"Come outa there, you goddamn hoople!" a burly uniformed cop shouted in at me and grabbed my collar. I scrambled out, grinning as idiotically as Mickey Rooney in *Sugar Babies*.

"Boy, am I glad to see you!" I said.

I looked at the mangled Lincoln, one demolished side cheek by jowl with a devastated police car and the other halfway through the hood of another one.

Cops were prying open the Lincoln, and out came a bloody, stunned, ruffled gorilla whose eyes were going around in circles. He couldn't have looked more helpless if biplanes had machine-gunned him off the top of the Empire State Building.

When the cops got Jennifer out of the Falcon and she only had a purple eye and whiplash, I sighed with relief. I didn't even care about the blood pouring down my forehead.

21

I WISH I COULD tell you I got a hero's welcome for bringing a murderous public menace to the Tenth Precinct on a silver platter. I wish I could say Detective Lawler recommended me for a Police Department civilian commendation. I wish I could even say that Ironhead Matthews gave me a bonus and a pat on the back. But the unhappy facts are that the ungrateful cops arrested me for reckless driving and destroying city property, and said they were suing the *Daily Press* for damages. This brought pitiful Charles W. Corcoran, the newspaper's lawyer, hopping over to the station house, frowning and tsk-tsking all the way. And when Ironhead got the complete, dreadful story, he transformed himself into Rumpelstiltskin and tried to tear himself apart. Even Jennifer was mad at me, although I'd saved her life. Sometimes I wonder why I didn't become a carpenter like my cousin Al.

The Ostrogoth in the mangled Lincoln was Sutty Larson, a beefy ox the size of a Pittsburgh Steeler lineman with a face fixed in a permanent, challenging sneer. When he came out of his daze, he wanted to say it was nothing but a fender-bender and let's forget the whole thing.

But there was the problem of the smashed cars for one thing, and Jennifer Ritter for another.

141

"That's the man who came to my apartment and tried to get money from me!" she told everyone at the Tenth Precinct.

"I never saw her before," Sutty moaned.

The cops patted Sutty down and came up with a .38 revolver, and then led him upstairs to the squad room. Jennifer and I were also taken upstairs, and the night-tour detective sergeant asked a few questions. As soon as he realized this was still more of Detective Jim Lawler's case, he called Lawler at home and told him the front of the station was littered with wrecked police vehicles and that it was his case. It was about two in the morning. I winced again.

A uniformed cop drove Jennifer and me to St. Clare's Hospital, where they examined us, took some X rays, and finally put three stitches in a cut on my forehead at the hairline. Jennifer needed some ice for her purple eye, and they told her to go see a doctor about her neck.

"Why didn't you tell me you were going to do that?" she complained as she looked stiff-necked into a mirror to examine her purple eye.

"Hell, I didn't know it myself until I did it," I said. "I ruined my car."

"Ruined your car!" she said, looking at me. "That piece of junk couldn't be ruined."

"Well, it did a job on Sutty," I said, and that finally made Jennifer smile through her pain.

When we got back to the Tenth Precinct squad room, Sutty wasn't looking so tough anymore. We saw him inside the squad room talking to Lawler, who appeared to be in a state of bleary exasperation. Sutty kept trying to avoid his eyes.

Sutty was in a jam, that was for sure. Lawler had his .38 and, as a ballistics test later showed, it was the weapon that killed Harry Berg. Even before they ran the test, though, Lawler knew it was the gun and so did Sutty.

Lawler came out of the squad room into the sergeant's office, where we were waiting, and his eyes were red-rimmed coals. He saw us and looked away, unable to bear the sight. He clamped accusing eyes on Sergeant McGee.

"Sarge," he said, speaking very carefully, "did you have to call me in on this? Couldn't you handle it?"

The sergeant made a face. "Jim, it looked like a train wreck out in front! We had a suspect with a .38. These people said it's your case."

Lawler hung his head and examined the top of Sergeant McGee's desk for a full second. He mumbled something uncomplimentary. Then he looked at me.

"Don't you ever spend a night at home?" he asked. He glanced back through the glass pane at Sutty, who was trying not to look at another detective who was questioning him.

"He's the one," Jennifer said. "I'll swear in front of fifty judges!"

"I know," said Lawler, running his hand through his reddish hair. "He admits it."

"He does?"

Lawler nodded. "Yes. But you're not going to like what he says."

Jennifer's face went pale, and she sat up straighter. "What did he say?"

Sutty's story as related by Lawler was curious, indeed. Caught as he was with a gun that killed somebody, his only chance was to cooperate and hope to plea bargain any charges against him down to lesser ones. Sutty had been the victim of an inside job, he complained. Somebody knew he had been skimming cash at Mulligan's and not reporting it to the IRS. "Hell, everybody does it," he explained.

Somebody also knew what was the closest thing on earth to Sutty's heart. One morning he was in Mulligan's checking his cash skim when the phone rang.

Lawler paused and glanced at us. "Somebody was on the phone and he said he had Sutty's kid."

Jennifer and I froze.

Larson's boy was a student at Xavier Military Academy. The voice said that young Alfred Larson was at that moment in a car with a gun at his head. To prove it, the boy was allowed to say one word: "Daddy!"

Then had come the message. A man would walk into Mulligan's within a few minutes. If Sutty wanted to see his son again, he would give that man $20,000 cash and cover it up with wine and ice. He would say nothing to the man, who was only a messenger.

"What could I do?" Sutty had said.

Jennifer was holding her face by now, and her shoulders were trembling.

"Howard Ritter?" I asked helplessly.

Lawler nodded and looked at Jennifer. "Didn't you say your father ran a couple of errands for a couple hundred each?"

Jennifer kept her hands over her face. She nodded her head yes.

Just as in the case of Sally Taliferro, the boy had heard nothing for a while except a car driving away. He eventually realized he was alone in the rented limousine, on the West Side by the Hudson River. He jumped out, ran to a phone, and called his father.

"When did this happen?" I asked.

"Two weeks before Ritter got shot," said Lawler.

The same pattern. Harry Berg couldn't go to the police about illegal gambling proceeds, and Sutty couldn't complain that skimmed cash had been stolen. The kidnapper had known a lot about both of them.

About three weeks later, Sutty had been cleaning his desk when he came across the *Daily Press* story and photograph about Ritter's death. He recognized Ritter, and went to the Irving Place apartment looking for revenge and his money. He found Jennifer.

"You were right that it was him," said Lawler.

Jennifer wasn't hiding her face anymore. She sat there dully, smoking and listening.

Sutty went back a second time, still full of murderous rage and looking for his money. He forced the apartment door open and waited inside. After a while, he fell asleep. That, apparently, was when he dropped the matches. He was awakened by a noise, and saw the apartment door open. A man was in the doorway, about to walk in.

Sutty insisted he had only said, "Who's that?" and the man in the doorway reached into his pocket. Sutty fired. It was Harry Berg.

"He claims self-defense," said Lawler wearily.

Jennifer was on her feet, pacing around, shaking her head. "It's crazy," she muttered. "The whole thing's crazy!"

"You still think your father wasn't in on it?"

"Absolutely not!"

"He's been identified in two kidnappings."

"I don't care!"

Lawler looked at me. "Sutty's boy told him the kidnapper wore a ski mask."

I was shaking my head. Lawler looked at me questioningly.

"Lawless, they pull two kidnappings for seventy thousand and Ritter settles for a couple hundred each time?"

"That's probably it," he came back. "They had a falling-out over money."

"No, no, no," said Jennifer miserably.

"I'm sorry," said Lawler, and walked into the lieutenant's office.

$\mathbf{W}$E CAME OUT UNDER the purple lights of the station house and I spotted my accordion-pleated Falcon angle-parked at the curb. The rear end was humped upward and the front end was smashed sideways. I was glad I hadn't poured hundreds into it for a valve job.

"How do you feel?" I asked Jennifer, who was fidgety and nervous.

"Hungry!" she said.

I realized we never had gotten any dinner at Mulligan's. It was about three in the morning. "How about some breakfast?"

She brightened a little and nodded. We walked over to Eighth Avenue and I hailed a cab, which drove us up to Forty-fifth Street to the Theatre Bar.

We slid into a booth and looked at the menu chalked on the big blackboard on the wall. Angie Pinzino strolled over, smiling his tired smile.

"There you are again," he said. "What'll it be?"

"Chili still hot?"

"Always."

I glanced at Jennifer. She nodded.

"Two," I said.

Then he noticed the bandage on my forehead and Jennifer's purple eye. "What happened?"

"Fender-bender," I said. "Don't ever back an old Ford into a new Lincoln."

"Not too smart," he agreed, and walked to the end of the bar to put in the food order. Then he came back with coffee for us.

"Getting anywhere?" he asked.

"Not exactly," I confessed, tired of the whole thing and anxious to talk about something else. "How about your boat?" I nudged Jennifer. "What do you think? Angie's buying a Staten Island ferryboat to turn into a floating nightclub."

Jennifer sat forward, enthralled. "What a good idea!" she chirped, apparently just as happy as I was to talk about something else.

Angie pulled the well-folded sheet of paper from his pocket, the notice of the city auction. He sighed, looking at the photo of the *Mae Murray* longingly.

"How much do you think it will cost?" I asked.

Angie wagged his head and winked elaborately. "Now, that's the joker. I don't know, exactly. Plenty."

"How much plenty? Ten thousand?"

Angie smiled at my ignorance. "That gets you the whistle."

"A hundred thousand?"

He got serious then. "Maybe double that."

I stopped eating my chili. "Two hundred thousand dollars?" I said, flabbergasted. "Did you hit the lottery?"

Angie laughed. "I'll have to sell this joint. Or at least mortgage the hell out of it. But I told Barney I'd get my half if he gets his."

"Barney Wells?" I asked stupidly.

"Yeah."

"Barney Wells is putting up a hundred thousand?" I said, my eyebrows challenging my hairline.

Angie shook his head and guffawed. "Hey, I didn't think he could do it, either. But I guess the kid's turned into a hot property. Cleaning up at some of the clubs around town, he told me."

Barney was making a hundred grand working at places like the Zebra Club, Mulligan's, and Going Up?

"That's where he's making the money, huh? At clubs around town?"

"Yeah, that's what he says. And Joycie's putting some in from her folks."

Joyce. That would be Barney's vacant-eyed girlfriend with the Empress Josephine hairstyle. I sat back against the booth, and my mind was swirling around in a new ticktacktoe game. I suddenly realized that Barney Wells's name had been popping up in a lot of interesting places. He had worked at the Zebra Club and Mulligan's. Now he was coming up with $100,000?

Angie was still talking about it. "Of course, we'll have to fix the boat up, and that'll cost too. But it's gonna be something! Angie Pinzino from Red Hook . . . maitre d'!" He was enjoying his future fantasy. "I'll be outa this greasy spoon for good."

"Sounds great," I agreed. "Captain Angelo."

"We haven't got much more time, though," Angie went on. "The kid's got to get his money together, and Joyce too. The auction's in about two weeks. September the thirteenth."

"Is Joyce going to work on the boat too?"

He sighed. "Yeah." Plainly he had his doubts about Joyce. "If she doesn't get *sick* again," he grimaced.

"Sick, huh?" I asked, and Barney looked away and shrugged.

"Yeah," he said softly. "She's been on something lately. Pills. I don't know why she started that."

"They live together?" I asked.

"Over on West Thirty-sixth. She was in the hospital, but I guess she's okay now." He shook his head.

Joyce's other-world eyes flashed into my consciousness. Pills. I had thought she was on something besides Scotch.

And then something else that Barney Wells had said popped into my mind.

"Anybody can do Bogart," he had told me.

149

23

YOU KNOW HOW IT is when there's something you're anxious to do right away but can't? That's the way I felt that early morning riding across town in a taxi with Jennifer. I wanted to get going on some of the questions that were tap-dancing in my mind about Barney Wells. But it was nearly four o'clock in the morning, and all I could do was sit there patiently in the dark cab with Jennifer leaning against me.

Jennifer was still in a floating funk. She pressed against me and held my hand, clinging to me as though her life depended upon it. Now that we were reasonably sure nobody else would be coming to her apartment on Irving Place with a gun, she had unaccountably decided to come back to my place.

"I can't be alone tonight," she murmured.

We got to East Eighty-second Street and went upstairs, and she didn't want me out of her sight or touch. She huddled against me in the bed, and held on tight, unable to get close enough.

"Don't let me go," she whispered.

"I won't."

When she finally dozed off, she would awaken with a quick movement and reach out to make sure I was still there. Then she would drop off again, awake again, and burrow against me. It's a good thing I wasn't able to sleep anyway.

Morning galloped through the windows in about twenty minutes, it seemed to me.

Jennifer didn't go to acting class that day because she had an appointment with a doctor about her whiplash. I left her sitting at the little table, and walked to the Lexington Avenue subway for the ride downtown to Forty-second Street. Going down the stairs, I started missing the Falcon already. Once inside a subway car with its ritualistic bear scrapings on the walls, I felt desolate without it. I was on a detour through Calcutta.

I came off the elevator and into the city room filled with plans to check up on Barney Wells, but I hadn't counted on the ambush. I should have, of course. There they were—Pitiful and Mount St. Helens—sitting in Ironhead's office waiting for me. Ironhead crooked his finger at me and I walked across the Bridge of Sighs to face them.

"Well, General Patton, I'm gratified you've honored us with your presence." That from Ironhead in an outburst of what he considered humor.

Charles W. Corcoran sat there looking out the window, shaking his head slowly, indicating he had no adequate words for this distressing situation.

I was going to ask, "What's the matter?" but felt any remark whatsoever would be construed as impudence. I waited.

"Well?" Ironhead at least declaimed portentously. Corcoran allowed himself a grave, disappointed, sorrowful glance at me too.

"Ironhead . . ." I started.

"Are you out of your mind?" he yelled, jumping up and leaning over the desk at me. "What are you doing about that goddamn four-car pile-up?"

"I don't know if my Falcon can be fixed or not," I said. "I may have to rent a car."

Ironhead's eyes popped and his mouth opened like a volcanic crater. "Your *Falcon*?"

Corcoran also rumbled an avalanche from his lofty legal pinnacle. "I have been in communication with the City Corporation Counsel's office," he pronounced. "The City of New York is going to sue you for destruction of city property."

"Me personally?"

"You surely don't imagine the demolition is the responsibility of this newspaper?" Corcoran gasped in indignation.

"But I was trying to get away from a killer!" I protested.

Ironhead started to speak, but an animal squawk came out. "Trying to get *away*?" he finally managed. "*Trying to get away!*" How in the name of clarity, the English language, and common decency could I call racing backward down a crowded, one-way street directly in front of a police station "trying to get away"? He wanted to know. How could slamming into a Lincoln Continental, smashing barbarously into fourteen parked City of New York Police Department radio cars worth forty or fifty thousand dollars each, possibly be considered anything except the drunken rampage of a General Patton gone berserk?

I felt like an insignificant gondolier facing the Council of Ten in the Doge's Palace in Old Venice. I remembered a famous editor on the old *New York Graphic*, possibly the most salacious of yellow sheets in New York City's history, in a similar situation. The publisher stormed up to him one day and shrieked, "Goddamn it, Emil, we now have libel suits against us for ten million dollars! What are you going to do about it?" Said the editor calmly, "Take it out of my salary." This caused me to smile slightly.

"You think this is funny?" Ironhead demanded. He had been studying my face like the way Rommel would read a topographical map of the Libyan Desert.

"No, Ironhead, and I didn't think it was funny when that NFL linebacker came after Jennifer and me with a gun, either. I was on a story!"

"I must strenuously object to that," Corcoran said, sitting

153

up sharply. He thought we were on trial already. Ironhead came stomping around his desk to get his red face up against mine.

"You were not on any story," he raged. "It was three o'clock in the fucking morning!"

"Listen, Barry Nicholson would have given me a bonus," I blurted out.

Ironhead flinched and drew back. Barry Nicholson was a legendary city editor for whom Ironhead had worked as a young reporter. If you stole a Fifth Avenue bus and crashed it into Police Headquarters to get a story, Barry Nicholson understood. In fact, if you *didn't* steal the bus, you were in trouble.

I didn't realize what a nerve I'd hit until Corcoran started dressing me down for "unauthorized depredations that this newspaper disclaims and totally rejects . . ."

"Aw, for chrissake, shut up," I heard Ironhead mumble.

"Pardon me?"

"Goddamn it, I'm getting sick and tired of the business and legal office telling me how to run my city room!"

"But Arnold . . ."

"Arnold?" I blurted out, and then remembered it was Ironhead's real name.

"I forgot. I did put him on the story," Ironhead muttered. He turned on me. "But I didn't tell you to bazooka the Tenth Precinct!"

"The thing is, I've got some hot leads now," I jumped in. "I just need a car— could I use a *Daily Press* radio car?"

Corcoran swayed back in his chair as though he were having a heart attack.

"A radio car?" Ironhead asked incredulously.

"Well, then, can I rent a car till mine gets fixed?"

"You won't need a car," said Ironhead. "You're back on rewrite. Arty Graves will handle the Berg story."

"It's not the Berg story, it's the Ritter story."

154

"He'll handle that too."

"But I'm really sailing now."

"Get out of here!"

Ironhead's face was red and contorted, and Corcoran's was a restrained, indignant mask. I decided to leave while I still could. When I got to the city desk, Jim Owens looked up. "You working for the city desk today?"

I nodded glumly.

"Good," he said. "Reilly's on vacation. I need a statue interview on some pigeons."

"What was that?"

"The pigeons are crapping all over the statue of Nathan Hale down by City Hall, and the pigeon lovers won't let the city kill them. So do a story from Nathan Hale's point of view about freedom and how patriots always get shit on in the end."

"Thanks."

"Get the pigeons' side, too. Make it sing, and don't get too dirty. This is a family newspaper."

There you have the high aspirations of the fourth estate. Here I had a murder and kidnapping boiling over, and the *Daily Press* wanted an interview with some pigeons. I sat at my typewriter, noodling away, trying to conjure up an imaginary conversation with Nathan Hale, but the face in my mind's eye resembled that of a pugnacious thug in a blue suit. I put in a call to Lawler.

"Well, if it isn't Demolition Derby."

"You're not really suing me," I asked sourly.

Lawler laughed. "*I'm* not. I don't know about the department."

"Listen, could you ask Sutty a question for me?"

"Afraid not. He's on the way downtown to arraignment."

"Great," I said. "Thanks."

So even Sutty was beyond my reach. I returned to Nathan Hale and his pigeons, but even as I tried out approaches to the story, my mind was running in other directions. I strolled over to the city desk.

"Hey, Owens, I have to go down to City Hall and talk to some people and have a look at the statue."

"Okay," he said, barely looking up. "Don't be long."

I scooted out of the city room as fast as I could, walked over to the Lexington Avenue subway, and headed downtown. It had occurred to me that Manhattan Criminal Court, where Sutty would be arraigned, was only a couple blocks up from City Hall.

I got off the subway and walked up to the old gray criminal-court building, where I walked through the scarred and cavernous marble lobby to the press room. Press rooms in criminal-court buildings used to be open for anyone to walk in and talk to the reporters. But that had all changed in recent years when the ink-stained wretches became practically prisoners in their little rooms because of the crazies who kept stomping in to demand stories about this or that or to upbraid reporters for what the crazies considered bias.

Anyway, I banged my fist on the press room door till Mickey Pearl, our courthouse reporter, opened it and looked out. When he saw it was me, he opened up and I went in.

"Hey, Mickey, I'm looking for an arraignment. Guy named Sutty Larson, on a murder charge."

Mickey's brain clicked, and he had it. "The Harry Berg thing that Ironhead's been yelling about?"

"Yeah. Larson's supposed to be arraigned this afternoon."

Mickey Pearl had covered Manhattan Criminal Court for a lot of years and knew the place inside and out. He was a cousin of Sandy Pearl, who had covered Manhattan Supreme Court, the civil court, down the street, until he got mixed up with some shady lawyers and ended up dead. But Mickey was as honest as his cousin Sandy had been crooked.

He put in a call to the DA's office upstairs, and then turned to me. "Arraignment, Part One," he said. "Are you going to file on this?"

"Don't count on me," I dodged. "I've got to do a pigeon story."

"Pigeons?" Mickey's pale eyes measured me to see if I were possibly pulling his leg—or had had too many Schaefers.

"Don't ask," I said, and headed out of the press room and down the marble corridor to A.P. One. I slid into a bench and waited.

Arraignment court is something like the Roman Coliseum must have been when they were putting lions and elephants in to fight Christians and Sarmatians. There are no perceptible rules except noise and confusion, and an irritated, frowning judge sits on a raised bench like a disgusted Nero. A sullen stream of glowering defendants—hookers, muggers, burglars, and accused killers—come in from a bullpen to a bench along one wall. They work their way to the end, where a Legal Aid lawyer whispers with them for a few minutes, and then they go before a harassed judge and a usually young and over-whelmed assistant district attorney. Unable to handle this flood, the system turns most of the defendants loose because it doesn't know what else to do. They walk out on low bail or no bail, never to be seen again until the next time they're arrested. Sometimes they're fined or sent to Rikers Island to await another court appearance.

Anyway, I waited until Sutty appeared at last at the end of the bench and worked his way along to go before the judge. A portly, scowling lawyer wearing rimless glasses popped up when Sutty's case was called. He hurried to the judge's bench and they held a whispered conference. Then the lawyer and Sutty walked out of the well of the court into the spectators' seats. Apparently Sutty's case was going onto the second calendar call, and he would be trying to make bail.

I moved across the aisle and slid into the spectator's bench beside them. "Hi," I said softly, "Ed Fitzgerald, *Daily Press*."

Rimless Glasses immediately plastered a professional smile on his face, always ready to talk to the press if it would get his name in the paper.

157

"Fred Knapp." He smiled.

Then Sutty Larson focused on me, and I thought he was going to lunge across the lawyer to choke me.

"Hey, that's the bastard that slammed into me," Sutty growled.

"Wait a minute, Sutty," I said. "I'm on your side."

Sutty's great, bony jaw fell. "*My* side?"

"What's this?" the lawyer interrupted.

Sutty glared at me, and I knew what it was like to stare into the eyes of a dinosaur. "You came after me, Sutty," I said as fast as I could. "I was only trying to get away. What would you have done?"

"You got me in a jam." He was sulking.

"Listen, I'm trying to find the guy who grabbed your kid."

The dinosaur eyes blinked. He frowned in confusion. "How'd you find out about that?"

"Never mind. I found out. That's what this case is all about."

"Mr. Larson, I would advise you not to talk to this man," Knapp said, annoyed at being ignored.

Sutty was still looking at me. "What do you want?"

"Did Barney Wells work at your club as a comic?"

Sutty cocked his head, remembering. "Yeah, he did."

"Did you pay him a lot of money?"

He recoiled and frowned. "Whaddya talking about? Hell, he was lousy."

"You didn't pay him big money?"

"I fired him after a week."

24

AS I WALKED OUT of the grimy criminal-court building, the smug face of Barney Wells was dancing before me. He kept turning up everywhere. He had worked at both the Zebra Club and Mulligan's, and now he was coming up with a pile of money to buy a ferryboat with Angie Pinzino.

If Barney was mixed up in this mess, he had managed to keep himself one step removed from everything. That step was Ritter, who wasn't around to explain.

But there was one other middleman who might be able to help. The mysterious, eccentric Mr. Goodman. Our Mr. Goodman must have been the guy in the cabin cruiser who fished up the red bag with the money in it. Because that's what the red bag had to be. I needed to find Mr. Goodman.

I walked over to City Hall and into Room Nine, the press room. Vinnie Eigen, the bureau chief for the *Daily Press*, looked up and gave me his choirboy smile.

"Hey, Fitz." He smiled tauntingly. "Nice of you to take over the pigeon-shit story."

"Go hump yourself."

"Ironhead's been on the phone asking if you got any good quotes out of Nathan Hale."

"He can hump himself too." Eigen laughed, delighted that he hadn't been stuck with it.

I got on the phone and called Information to see if there was a listing for the Seventy-ninth Street Boat Basin. There was, but the operator had no telephone listing for a Mr. Goodman.

"Are there any boats there with phones that have unlisted numbers?"

"If it's unlisted, I couldn't tell you," the information operator said.

I called the boat basin and got the dockmaster on the line. No, he said, he had no telephone for a boat owner named Mr. Goodman.

"Do you know if any of the boat owners have unlisted numbers?"

"I think some of them, yes."

"Well, do you have a list of people who have boats in the basin?" I asked.

Yes, of course, he had a listing. "Who you looking for?"

"Mr. Goodman."

"I got no Mr. Goodman."

I hung up and spat something vile.

"Tsk-tsk," said Vinnie through a cherubic smile. "Those are not words found in the bright lexicon of youth."

I walked outside, down the City Hall steps, and past Nathan Hale's statue. I noticed that the pigeons, totally unimpressed by City Hall's campaign to drive them into exile, were fluttering about, cooing, and dumping on our patriot as usual.

I hailed a cab, still mourning my crippled green Falcon, and told the driver to take me to the boat basin. We headed north up the West Side along the Hudson River, past crumbling old piers and the U.S.S. *Intrepid* to the cobblestoned Henry Hudson Parkway. At Seventy-ninth Street the cabbie got off and curved around under the parkway into a traffic circle beside the boat basin. We drove down a curving ramp into a dark, underground garage. I paid him, asked him to wait, and walked out onto the asphalt pathway in front of the boat basin.

There was a high wire fence between the pathway and the

basin, an iron-and-wire gate in the fence, and a blue and white sign by the gate: 79TH ST. MARINA. PRIVATE DOCK. BOAT OWNERS ONLY. I tried the gate, but it was locked.

Through the wire gate I could see boats lined up in the marina. Houseboats, yachts, cabin cruisers, sailboats, and catamarans.

"Hey!" I yelled and rattled the gate. Nothing.

I saw a Coke bottle on the ground beside the gate, and flung it high up over the fence so that it landed on the wooden roof of the dockmaster's low shed. The bottle went *clunk* on the roof, and then rolled off into the water with a small splash.

A head popped out of the shed. "Who did that?" it shouted angrily.

"Hey!" I called. "I have to talk to you. Just came from City Hall."

The face reacted with interest, and a round, flabby body attached to it wearing red plaid shorts, emerged from the shed and waddled along the wooden boardwalk to the wire gate. He looked at me through the wire fence.

"You the dockmaster?"

"Must have stepped out," he said. "What can I do for you?"

"You're his assistant?"

"Naw. I got a boat here."

"Just came from City Hall, and they asked me to come up and look the place over," I said. I took out my wallet and opened and closed it.

"You guys finally gonna dredge the marina?" he asked, opening the iron gate. "We'll be sticking to the bottom soon." I quickly stepped inside.

"I'm supposed to look it over," I said, inventing as well as I could. "A guy named Goodman who has a boat here called us."

The flabby boat owner frowned at that. "Goodman? What kind of boat?"

"I was hoping you could show me," I said. "You know who has boats here?"

"I know most of them. The dockmaster ought to be back pretty soon." He waddled back down the boardwalk ahead of me, saying the name over and over. "Goodman . . . doesn't ring a bell . . . Goodman . . ."

He reached the low shed and went inside with me following on his heels. "Let's see here," he muttered, and went to a large cardboard chart on the wall. There was a list of boat owners for the 110 slips in the marina. He started looking it over, and I was looking over his shoulder.

"Goodman," he was saying, looking down the list. But I could see there was no Goodman among the Gs on the big chart. I was about to give it up, when a name leaped out at me from near the bottom.

B. Wells.

"B. Wells," I said. "Is that Barney Wells?"

The boat owner gave me a sideways glance. "Yeah."

"You know him?"

The flabby gentleman reached into the pocket of his red plaid shorts and took out a crumpled pack of cigarettes. He took one out and lighted it, studying me. "Yeah, I know him."

"What kind of a boat does he have?"

"Chris Craft," he said. "Twenty-six footer. I thought you said Goodman. What do you want with Wells?"

"Personal," I said.

Plaid Shorts smiled knowingly. "He owe you money? Or did he steal your girl?" Barney had a nice reputation.

"Is that an expensive boat?" I asked.

The dumpy man actually smiled, though with derision. "That wooden bucket? Hell, it's twenty years old, at least. Few thousand down."

"Does it cost a lot to keep a boat here?"

"Slippage is thirty bucks a foot. Cheaper than rent."

"Is Wells paid up?"

"I think he is now."

That got my attention. "He wasn't before?"

"I heard he was about six months behind, is all," he smiled. "They were going to toss him out."

"Could you show me his boat?"

He dragged on his cigarette and examined me. "You a cop?"

"I told you . . . personal."

He grunted. "No skin off my nose. Number thirty-seven."

"Thanks," I said, and turned to leave.

"I knew there was something funny about that guy," he offered, leaning on the counter.

"Why?"

"He talks like a big shot, acts like a big shot, and has a cheap boat. You can always tell." His face spread into a self-satisfied smile.

I walked out of the shed and along the floating walkways between the moored boats. After retracing my steps a couple of times, I found slip thirty-seven. The boat was an old wooden cabin cruiser in need of a paint job. There was nobody aboard. I was walking back toward the dockmaster's office when I looked back and noticed the name across the stern: *The Boffo*.

To get out of the marina, you walk back past the dockmaster's wooden shed and up the wooden walkway to the wire gate. Then you cross an asphalt path and go into the underground garage. When I got there, the yellow cab had left, of course.

I walked up the curving ramp and through the traffic circle, going under the Henry Hudson Parkway to Riverside Drive. A lot of cabs went by, but none of them stopped. I walked down Seventy-ninth Street to West End Avenue, but finally had to go over to Broadway before I could get a cab.

Riding downtown, my head was a meteor racing through intergalactic space, colliding with other space debris. The first collision gave off the message that there was no Mr. Goodman. There was only Barney Wells.

It was Barney Wells as Humphrey Bogart who had hired

Howard Ritter to go to the Zebra Club and to Mulligan's to pick up ransom money.

It was Barney Wells driving *The Boffo* who followed the riverboat and picked up the red bag. I had no doubt now that the $20,000 ransom Sutty Larson paid to Ritter for the freedom of his son also was eventually tossed off the stern of the excursion boat and picked up by Wells in *The Boffo*.

I sat there in the bouncing cab, congratulating myself, until I heard a flat note creep in. A sour dissonance was getting through to me.

I realized that if Barney were on *The Boffo*, then he hadn't been aboard the riverboat with Ritter.

Barney had to be responsible for Ritter's murder, but he hadn't been on the scene. My elation slid down the scale into a blaring raspberry of honking tubas.

I had set out to prove that Barney Wells had to have been aboard the riverboat to kill Ritter. Now I had proved that he couldn't have been.

When I paid the cabby and slammed the door, it thumped through me like a big bass drum.

25

BACK IN THE *Daily Press* city room, I wrote a story about
Nathan Hale and his feathered friends, but my mind was a
million miles away. Barney Wells was smarter than I had
thought, but he wasn't as smart as *he* thought. Somehow, he
had conned Howard Ritter into the first messenger job, when
Sutty was taken for $20,000. But something had gone wrong
on the second job, the Harry Berg one. Maybe Jennifer's
yelling at her father had caused him to ask questions. Maybe
he realized there had to be more than wine in that bag. Barney
had set him up very carefully, all right, having him make those
earlier, innocent wine deliveries to "Mr. Goodman" at the
Central Park concert and to the observation deck at the World
Trade Center. Those two had to be practice runs, to persuade
Ritter that he was, indeed, working for a harmless, wealthy
old eccentric.

What had happened on the stern of the boat? Did Ritter
open the bag and find the money? If he did, somebody was
nearby watching him. When Ritter decided to figure out what
was going on, somebody decided to put a bullet into him.

It had to have been Barney Wells. But it couldn't have been
if Wells were on *The Boffo* following the riverboat.

These are the kind of opposites that drive a reporter to

Costello's and into several mugs of beer. There was something on the edge of my consciousness that I was trying to dredge up. All I dredged up was the last of the mug of beer. I finally decided the hell with it and called Jennifer at East Eighty-second Street to find out how she was doing with her pain in the neck. There was no answer, so I tried her apartment.

I don't know about you, but I detest these goddamn machines that answer people's phones. There came Jennifer's disembodied voice: "I'm not home right now, but if you'll leave your name and number, I'll be sure to get back to you. Please wait for the beep."

I never wait for the beep, and I didn't this time either. I strolled back from the pay phone to my barstool, past the Thurber cartoons on the wall, and ordered another mug.

"Goddamn machines," I muttered, and as soon as the words were out, it hit me. Recording machines! Humphrey Bogart's voice was on Jennifer's telephone recording machine. I hurried back to the phone booth and called the Tenth Precinct.

"Lawless," I said, "it's Fitz."

"Well, well, if it isn't Demolition Derby himself," he said jovially.

"Thanks. Listen, I got it figured out."

"Yeah?" said Lawler. "You mean how to get out of the lawsuit?" He was having a good time.

"No, no, damn it, the Ritter case."

"Oh, that."

"Yes. 'Oh, that.' One of the comics we were with the night Berg got it is the guy we want. Barney Wells. He's Ski Mask."

Lawler sighed heavily. "Very good. I suppose you have something to back that up?"

"You bet I have."

"Evidence?"

"Damn right, evidence. How about that voice print you used to clear Trigger Moran? Wells has to be the one who called Ritter and hired him, and Jennifer's telephone recorder got it."

"Hmmm," said Lawler. "Can you get this Wells to say the same words into a tape for us?"

I paused. "Well . . . hell . . . I don't know. Probably not, if he's really Ski Mask. Would he have to say the same words? Isn't a voice print as good as fingerprints?"

"Yeah, about as good," said Lawler. "You can hardly ever convict anybody with either one."

"What do you mean? How about Trigger Moran?"

Lawler sighed. "Moran cooperated. We didn't have much of a case on him, anyway. But if you want to take a voice print into court, they're usually not worth a damn. You can hardly get them into evidence, and they have to be perfect. This one's a scratchy telephone recording out of a Crackerjack box."

"But it's him, Lawless! He's a comic, and he told me he can do Bogart."

"That's another thing," Lawler went on. "The voice on that damned recording sounds like . . . I don't know what . . . a fairy."

"Well, Bogart lisped a little, and he was imitating him."

"The voice is practically a whisper, and whispers don't record well. You lose, I don't know, a thousand cycles if you whisper."

"Cycles?"

"Yes, cycles! A voice print is a spectograph of your voice, and it has to be perfect to get it into evidence. If you can get it in at all. If it's on a damned two-dollar recorder, it's crap. And if the voice is a whisper, it's less than crap."

So much for my wonderful brainstorm.

"Thanks, Lawless. I'm going to put you in for P.C. some day."

"You're welcome."

On the way home, I picked up a few things at the supermarket on the corner. When I let myself in, Jennifer was there at the tiny kitchen table. She was sitting as straight and stiff as a statue of Cleopatra. Around her neck and cupping her chin was one of those pink surgical neck brace collars.

167

You might think a surgical collar would limit one's field of vision, but you would be wrong. No matter where I moved, Jennifer's brown, pain-filled eyes followed me. Not even her cascading India-ink hair covered the collar.

"Hurt?" I asked idiotically.

"Oh, no," she said unmovingly. "Why should it hurt just because I can't move?"

"How long do you have to wear it?"

"It's already been thirty years."

"Sorry. But, listen, wait till you hear what I found out today. There's no Mr. Goodman!"

I got the idea that words also were a pain to her, because she closed her eyes and seemed to be trying to pull her head down into the collar.

"Fitz," she said, and it was a plea for mercy. "Please don't tell me any more."

"What?"

"I don't believe I could stand one more word about it. I feel I'm a fraction of an inch from disintegrating. I was just about to leave."

"Leave?"

"I'm moving back home." She took out a cigarette and held it up straight in front of her face parallel to the table. She carefully raised her cigarette lighter to the tip and concentrated mightily on setting fire to it.

I said something inspired like "Oh."

"I want to thank you," she said slowly, and it sounded like a Manhattan State Supreme Court Justice about to pronounce sentence on a mugger. "I know you mean well. I know I kept at you to do something. And I appreciate it. I really do."

She puffed on her cigarette, moving with careful precision to bring it to her mouth. It was a delicate, programmed undertaking.

"But I . . . you see . . ." She fluttered her dark eyelashes, blinking back the tears that were threatening, and paused

168

until the danger passed. "It isn't meant to be. The system doesn't work. Because nobody cares."

"I care."

She closed her eyes, let out a breath, opened them again. "It costs too much." She stood up, straight and stiffly and cautiously. "I have to go."

I walked her downstairs and to Second Avenue, where she got a cab. She sat on the edge of the seat, holding handles on both sides, and when the cab started she didn't look back. I guess she couldn't.

Those are the things that torment you. Nobody thinks about the people who are left behind when somebody gets killed. For them, it's never over. It just recedes inside and becomes an instinct of fright, an ever-present, immobilizing spot of unavenged rage. I was afraid the lively fire that once flashed in Jennifer's eyes had become permanently a tiny pilot light.

The two steaks I had brought home, over which I was going to regale Jennifer with my latest discoveries, went in on top of the ice-cube trays. I opened a can of Campbell's bean-and-bacon soup, and ate it with some rye bead and butter. I sprawled on the couch, picked up *The Complete Works of Tacitus*, and browsed through the ancient Roman historian's account of the life of Agricola. "Let it be known to those whose habit it is to admire the disregard of authority, that there may be great men even under bad emperors," was Tacitus's declaration to me.

It was a long night, during which I slept fitfully, awaking over and over in anxiety and confusion, wondering where I was. I marched with Cnaeus Julius Agricola through Britain, and returned with him to Rome when he was recalled by the jealous Emperor Domitian. Summoned before a scowling Domitian, Agricola was informed that augurs had studied the flight of pigeons over the Emperor's statue in the Forum and determined that they were profaning Domitian at Agricola's command.

The grave emperor ranted and stormed and condemned the innocent Agricola to death "on the false Ides," unless he could solve the riddle: "How did base emperors past turn seven into nine?"

Somehow it was up to me to give Agricola the answer and save his life. But as one is always helpless in a dream, I couldn't, and the doom described by Tacitus ("The prevalent rumor was that he was destroyed by poison") implacably occurred. Only after what Tacitus called this "deplorable calamity" did I realize the solution to Domitian's riddle.

Something about September had always troubled me. It had always struck me as incongruous that beginning with September, the months have crazy names. September is the ninth month even though it means, literally, the "seventh" month, and October, November, and December mean literally the eighth, ninth, and tenth months. When Julius Caesar reorganized the Old Roman calendar, the last two months, January and February, became the first two months. The Roman Senate changed the name of the fifth month, Quinctilis, to July in Caesar's honor, and later the Emperor Augustus changed the sixth month, Sixtilis, to August. But it was the ill-named September that always got me.

So the "false Ides" running around in my head was September the thirteenth. Some people think the ides always fell on the fifteenth, but that was only in March, May, July, and October. In all the other months, it was on the thirteenth.

I got up and walked out into the living room to stare out over the street. I was too restless to sleep. On September the thirteenth, the *Mae Murray* would be auctioned off, and by that date Barney Wells needed all of his $100,000. If my calculations were right, he had only $70,000.

That was what Domitian and Tacitus and Agricola were trying to tell me. Beware the Ides of September.

26

AFTER THAT, I WAS able to sleep. But my unconscious was still active, because when I awoke and put on some tea, I found myself looking at the calendar. September the thirteenth—the Ides of September—was on a Thursday. I realized that the previous two kidnappings had been staged on Fridays, and saw that today was the only Friday left before the Ides.

I put in a call to Big Jim Lawler, but he wasn't available. I shaved and dressed and walked outside to hail a cab to the Tenth Precinct. When I climbed the stairs to the detective squad room, Lawler and the other detectives were in with the sergeant, going over their cases for the day.

I pounced on Lawler the moment he came out, and walked to his desk with him. "Listen," I started.

"For chrissake, Fitz," he moaned, "I haven't even had coffee yet."

"Lawless, it's Friday."

Lawler nodded his head at this profound deduction. "You've got detective blood in you."

"He's going to pull another this morning," I said.

"Is that so?" He opened a plastic cup of coffee on his desk and sipped it. "Why do they always bring it when I'm in with the sarge?"

"Dammit, will you listen?" I complained. "Both of the other

jobs were on Fridays. He needs the rest of the money by next Thursday. Today is it."

He shook his head. "You lost me."

I started talking and wouldn't stop until I'd told him what I had come up with. Detectives are plenty skeptical and even stubborn, but they know that criminals follow routines. If it works, they'll do it again. If criminals always staged their jobs in brand-new ways, they'd be extremely hard to catch. Hell, they're hard to catch anyway. But Lawler was listening as I argued that Ski Mask would pull the same kind of stunt again and that this was the day.

"Providing you're right that Barney Wells is the guy," he said doubtfully.

"Got to be."

"Why?"

"Okay, one: He worked for the Zebra Club and he worked at Mulligan's. So he knew a lot about both of them."

"That's it?"

"No. Number two: He wants his own place, see? A ferry-boat."

Lawler shot a look at me. "A ferryboat? What the hell for?"

"To turn it into a nightclub. He's got big ideas!"

"He's a punk comic."

"To you. To himself, he's Alexander Cohen."

"Who's Alexander Cohen?"

"He thinks he's Napoleon! Will you get your fist out of your grumper!" I could see Lawler didn't like it that I was on his turf telling him his business. It couldn't be helped.

"He needs a hundred thousand dollars by the Ides of September."

"The what?"

"Sorry. September thirteenth. He's told people he got the money from those two nightclubs where he worked, but he got fired from both places."

Lawler leaned across the desk, put his elbows up, and lighted a cigarette. "Yeah?" It was nice to see the lanky detective paying attention. It made me realize something I hadn't picked up on before.

"Revenge!" I blurted. "You know what he's doing? He's getting the money for his own nightclub from the very guys who canned him!"

I leaned back and lighted a Tiparillo. All of a sudden, a lot of things made sense. Barney Wells sounded like somebody I'd read about once in an article about narcissism.

"Hey," I said, standing up restlessly, "that other joint fired him, too."

"What other joint?"

"The one on West Forty-ninth Street. Going Up. He said he quit, but that's it! They must have fired him too."

"You know where it is?" said Lawler.

"Sure. Near Seventh Avenue."

Lawler was on his feet. "Rocco," he called, and his partner Santelli looked up from the report he was typing.

"Let's go," said Lawler.

I followed them down the stairs and into a squad car. Santelli shot over to Eighth Avenue and then north uptown to Forty-ninth Street. I spotted the place near the corner.

"There it is," I yelled. Santelli whipped the squad car to the curb in front of it. We hopped out and walked into the club. Right away, it was obvious something was up.

A plump, middle-aged guy in a red vest with a balding head saw us and came charging out of his office near the bar. His name popped into my head.

"Mr. Vergari?" I asked.

Vergari stopped and looked us over with eyes like saucers. He was as nervous as somebody who just walked away from a plane crash.

"What do you want? Who are you?" he demanded.

"Are you Vergari?" Lawler said, flashing his shield. "Detective Lawler."

Vergari looked at the shield, swallowed and exhaled, and said, "Yeah, yeah."

173

"Look, Vergari," said Lawler, "I haven't got time to explain, but if somebody's trying to extort money from you, you'd better tell us."

Vergari looked stunned, as though somebody had stuck a knife between his ribs.

"Is somebody coming here to collect ransom?" Lawler asked. Vergari sank onto a barstool and grabbed his ears in his hands.

"Whatever's going down, we're going to find out about it," Lawler pressed him. "Better help us."

Vergari looked up. "He just walked out the door!"

"Who did?"

"Some guy. I don't know. They got my wife!"

Lawler kept his eyes on Vergari but talked to Santelli. "Rocco, call in. Tell Sarge to get somebody over here. Now, Vergari," he went on, "tell me what else you can."

"I tell you, that's all I know! Some bastard called me on the phone and said he'd be here. Before I could even think, he walked in. He walked out ten, fifteen minutes ago."

"Did you ask him anything?"

Vergari shook his head quickly. "They told me not to if I wanted to see Helen again! You know who the son-of-a-bitch is?"

Lawler looked away. "I'm not sure. Maybe." Santelli came walking back.

"They're on the way," said Santelli.

"Vergari, you come with us," said Lawler, starting out.

"No, no, I can't," he yelled in terror. "I've got to wait for a call from Helen. That bastard told me to stay by the phone."

"Okay," said Lawler. "Stay put. There are officers on the way here now. If you get a call before they arrive, contact the Tenth Precinct." He jotted down the number.

"All right," said Vergari.

"How much did you give him?"

Vergari made a face and held his ears again. "Thirty thousand."

"Why didn't you call the cops?" I asked Vergari, but he just sat there holding his ears and shaking his head.

"Couldn't, could you, Vergari?" Lawler said with not much sympathy. "You're dealing coke and pot out of here, aren't you?"

Vergari tried to shut it out with his hands. Lawler looked at me. "We knew it, but haven't been able to nail him. Looks like somebody else knew it too." But there was no time to worry about Vergari's little side trade at the moment.

Lawler and Santelli ran out the door to their squad car, and I was right behind them. We headed across Forty-ninth Street to the West Side Highway. I checked my watch. It was already after ten. Santelli put a flashing light on the roof and hit the siren at intersections. He wheeled the squad car onto the River Cruises parking lot, spewing gravel, but I could already see the excursion boat clearing the pier and sliding into the river.

"Shit," muttered Lawler. At the same time he was on the police radio, asking the harbor squad to meet him at Pier Eighty-one with a police launch.

I jumped from the car and ran across the parking lot to Twelfth Avenue, searching for a limousine. There it was, parked on Fortieth Street just up from Twelfth Avenue. Santelli was right behind me. The big black limo was empty, one of the rear doors standing open. There was a blanket on the floor of the backseat, and a car telephone in front.

There was no sign of Mrs. Vergari. Like Taffy, she'd been abandoned, and she'd left the scene.

"Gone," I said disconsolately.

Santelli was waving me away. "Keep your hands off the car," he commanded.

When I looked back at Pier Eighty-one, I saw Lawler hurrying across the parking lot toward the riverboat slip. Then I saw it—a harbor squad police launch coming in toward the pier. I took off, dashing across Twelfth Avenue through traffic, getting honked at and sworn at by drivers.

I got to the side of the pier as Lawler was climbing aboard, and jumped on behind him, practically knocking him down.

"Hey!" he shouted, and turned to see who it was. "Jesus, Fitz, would you jump into my grave that quick?"

I was too winded to answer. The police launch revved up, swung into a curve, and headed toward the river. Then it took off at high speed into the Hudson, swerved north, leaving a violent foamy wake, and drew a bead on the excursion boat ahead of us.

It didn't take long for the powerful launch to catch the big riverboat and draw up on the port side. Somebody radioed the boat. It slowed and we pulled in next to it.

"Stay here," Lawler told me, getting ready to jump from the launch onto the boat.

"In a pig's patoot," I said.

He scrambled across the riverboat, and once more I was behind him onto the deck so quickly that I was almost riding him piggyback.

"Get off me," he shouted as we both came crashing onto the boat amidships. He turned around and glared at me. "You're getting to be a pain in the butt."

I ignored him. There was no way I was going to be left out now. The riverboat speeded up again, and most of the passengers probably didn't even realize we had joined them.

Lawler conferred with the youthful purser. I slid around a corner and walked swiftly toward the stern into the cafeteria area, which was almost deserted.

There in the stern booth sat a man holding a red bag with a walkie-talkie in his hand. I moved closer, slowly, trying not to draw his attention. And then I saw somebody else in another booth watching the man with the red bag.

I looked closer, moving nearer and trying to make an identification. After a few more steps, there was no doubt. I stopped, but it was too late. I had been seen.

I kept walking slowly onward. Then I saw a hand come out of the raincoat and the handgun was pointing at me.

176

"Don't come any closer."

Blank eyes and a trembling hand. I kept walking. The gun shook and more words came, disorganized and undecipherable.

And then she took a step away from me and fainted onto the deck, the gun clattering across the floor. Joyce the waitress.

27

My TIMING WAS PERFECT, as usual. By the time Big Jim Lawler came trotting back to the stern, he saw me kneeling over Joyce.

"Goddamn it, now what have you done?" he wanted to know, squatting down beside the collapsed waitress. "Is she dead?"

"I didn't say a word to her, Lawless. She took one look at me and keeled over."

The guy in the stern booth was watching us both by now with a look of white-faced fright on his pinched little face. He probably thought we were boat hijackers.

Once Lawler was satisfied the woman on the deck wasn't dead, he got up and approached the bewildered, cowering shrimp in the booth. He flashed his detective's shield.

"Police," he said. "Would you please show me some identification?"

The little man looked at him through octagonal rimless glasses as though transformed into stone. Then he blinked and said, "What?"

"Police officer," said Lawler. "What are you doing on this boat?"

Octagonal Glasses gulped, looked at Joyce, who was starting to moan, and then searched Lawler's eyes. "I don't know anything," he finally squeaked. "I'm just delivering this bag." He indicated the red bag on the table in front of him.

"Delivering it where?"

In answer, Squeaky lifted a walkie-talkie he was holding in his right hand. "I don't know. He said he'd let me know."

Lawler took the walkie-talkie and examined it. He activated it and listened, but nothing was coming in.

Squeaky finally got his wallet out and was showing identification, still allowing his eyes to stray over toward Joyce and me.

"Stanley Jamison," he stammered. "I'm a messenger. Campbell's Messenger Service." He shoved four pieces of identification at Lawler, looking at Joyce again. "Is she all right?"

Joyce sat up, and I helped her onto a seat in a booth. She held her face in both hands and was trembling.

Lawler examined the red bag and unzipped it. He saw two bottles of Garibaldi Soave on a bed of ice.

"It's just white wine," said the messenger.

"Look under the ice," I told Lawler.

He lifted out the bottles of Garibaldi and scraped away the ice. Under the ice he found a plastic bag, which he lifted out and put on the table. Inside were stacks of cash.

"Wine, huh?"

Jamison looked positively stupefied. "Where'd that come from?"

Joyce shook her head and stared fuzzily across the table at me. "Oh, my God," she chirped weakly. "Oh, my God."

"What's going on?" I asked her. "What are you doing here?"

She rolled her head around, blinking her vacant Orphan Annie eyes and dug her hands into her already chaotic Josephine hair. She seemed to be trying to figure out where she was.

"I don't know what you mean," she finally said very unsteadily. She was only about half present.

Lawler finished looking over the messenger's ID, and then he leaned over to put his face close and said in a gruff, threatening salvo, "Listen, Jamison, you're in a lot of trouble.

You have the right to remain silent. You are entitled to contact counsel. Anything you say can and will be used against you in a court of law . . ."

Stanley Jamison's mouth popped open. He shoved himself back against the stern as far as possible. He understood what it meant when a cop reads you your rights.

"I didn't do anything!" he wailed.

"Where were you delivering this money?"

"I didn't know it was . . . I was . . . I don't know! He said he'd let me know."

Lawler picked up the walkie-talkie again.

"On this thing?" he asked.

Jamison nodded energetically.

Then static crackled on the walkie-talkie. Lawler jerked, startled, and almost dropped it. He put his ear closer and listened. He pushed the "send" button to transmit.

"Yes, this is Campbell's," he said into the radio.

Across from me, Joyce focused at last. She sat rigidly, her eyes glued on Lawler and the radio. She was also darting looks past Lawler toward the river.

"Okay," Lawler said, suddenly standing up. "Where?"

The detective turned and peered over the stern at the river, sweeping his gaze across it. I hopped up and went over to look too. Off to the starboard stern in the spray and the hard reflection of sunlight on the water, I saw a white cabin cruiser gaining on the excursion boat, its prow cutting the waves in a whitening furrow.

I motioned to Lawler to release the "talk" button on the walkie-talkie so my voice wouldn't go over the radio, and then pointed downriver.

"There it is—*The Boffo!*"

Lawler squinted into the sunlight and the glare and spotted it. He spoke into the walkie-talkie again. "Okay," he said, "got it."

Lawler put the walkie-talkie down. He put the two bottles of Garibaldi Soave back into the red bag, but left the money on the Formica tabletop. He zipped the bag shut and slid open the stern window.

"What did he tell you to do?" Lawler asked the pole-axed messenger.

"Huh?" he squealed. "Uh . . . hold it over the side and pull this cord."

Lawler shoved the red bag out the window and pulled the cord. With a smart *whoosh*, the red bag popped full of air, and he let it go.

The red bag bobbed in the wake of the riverboat, disappeared, and then popped up again in the frothy foam. The old wooden Chris Craft curved to port and reached the bag. We could see somebody on board fish it out with a gaff. Then the boat turned and started back down the river.

Lawler was already on his own, more powerful two-way police radio, directing the harbor-squad police launch to go after *The Boffo*.

The police launch's high, whining engines could be heard right away over the dull throb of the excursion boat. In a moment, we saw the launch peel off and hum into a graceful curve, churning a deep trough in the river and racing prow-up back downriver. The old wooden cabin cruiser had not a chance. The launch closed on *The Boffo*, siren screaming, and was soon alongside. Cops jumped from the launch onto the cruiser, and pretty soon Lawler heard a harbor-squad sergeant on his walkie-talkie.

"We have apprehended the perp," the sergeant said.

When the police launch came back alongside the riverboat, and we scrambled back aboard, I saw the lovely sight of Barney ("Mr. Goodman") Wells in handcuffs, sitting slumped in the forward compartment. He looked at me with an expression that would have blown the bottom out of the Battleship Maine.

28

I WISH I COULD tell you Barney Wells caved in, now that he had been caught in flagrante delicto, as Cicero would have said. The last thing I expected was injured protestations of innocence.

"What's this all about?" he demanded with indignation worthy of Willie Sutton.

"I'll bet you could tell us," Lawler replied calmly as the harbor-squad launch zoomed us back to Pier Eighty-one.

"Well, I'm sorry, but I don't understand a goddamn thing about this," he snapped. "I hope you know there are laws against false arrest!"

"Never mind the horseshit," Lawler said, losing his patience. "We've got the money, the gun, your girlfriend, and your messenger."

"My what?" Barney sneered with elaborate disdain.

"Why'd you fish that bag out of the river?"

"Because I saw it floating by, that's why," Wells spat out.

He was quite magnificent in his protestations. I was really amazed. "What's the matter with you, Barney?" I asked. "Don't you see it's all over?"

"I don't see anything at all," he snapped. "What do you think you've got me on?"

I looked at Lawler, and his troubled face told me it was a good question. We all rode down to the Tenth Precinct and walked up into the squad room, and I was feeling a little less cocky the more I thought about it. What could Wells be charged with? The question was mussing Lawler's face and my head.

As usual, the only one who would talk was the one who knew the least. Stanley Jamison, the terrified messenger, never stopped spilling his guts from the moment Lawler read him his rights. His endless spiel amounted to a plea that he was only a messenger.

All he knew was that he had received a telephone call at the Campbell's Messenger Service and had been asked if he would like to earn some extra money as a confidential messenger for a Mr. Goodman. Since it was confidential, the pay would be commensurate. In fact—$200.

Needless to say, like Barkis, Stanley Jamison was willing.

All he had to do, he was told, was to "follow the instructions in the red bag." Before he could ask anything more, the phone call had ended.

He had found a red bag on his doorstep, and inside were $100 in cash, brief instructions, and a walkie-talkie. The instructions told him to go to Going Up and pick up a package. He was to take the package down to the Hudson River Cruises excursion boat, go aboard, and wait to be contacted by Mr. Goodman. If he followed all the instructions, a second $100 would be mailed to his home.

Stanley Jamison had done as he was told—until police came running up to him, waving guns and accusing him of all sorts of felonies.

"Mr. Jamison," Lawler asked him, his eyes narrowing with scornful doubt, "didn't you wonder why you were being paid $200 for one errand?"

"Well, he told me why."

"Why?"

"Because it was confidential."

"Can you think of *any* errand, even a confidential one, that would be worth $200?" he asked levelly.

"What if it was diamonds?" asked Jamison excitedly. "Or

. . . blueprints? You need a professional messenger for those things. I'm a professional," he said proudly.

Lawler shook his head disgustedly.

Jamison looked at the floor. "We only make minimum wage, you know," he said then. "Where else could I make that kind of money for an errand?" He looked up defensively. "These things happen! How was I supposed to know?" he pleaded.

The messenger's story filled in some holes, all right, but it still didn't link the job directly to Wells.

"Can you identify the voice of the person who called you?" Lawler asked him.

"Yes," he said excitedly. "It was a funny voice. Let me think . . . some old movie star."

Lawler sighed. "Humphrey Bogart?"

"No, not him," said Jamison. "The other one. He always said, 'You dirty rat.' "

"James Cagney?" I asked in surprise.

"That's it! See, I can identify him!"

"Did you by any chance record the voice?" I asked hopefully. Lawler rolled his eyes heavenward.

"No," he said. "I never thought to."

So Barney had slightly changed his routine, probably because he had to improvise, and time was running out. He used a real messenger and a different voice.

"Does that help?" Jamison said hopefully. "I didn't do anything."

"It's up to the district attorney," said Lawler, and Jamison put his head on the desk and started bawling.

Of course when Lawler asked Wells if he wished to give a statement, Barney said he wanted a lawyer. "I'm gonna sue you for false arrest," he said.

"Go on," said Lawler, "make your phone call."

Wells went to the phone, pulled a card out of his wallet, and made a phone call. He was well prepared.

The key to the whole mess, of course, was Joyce Warner the waitress, who had been caught with a murder weapon in her

185

hand and no way out. But it was clear from the beginning that she wouldn't blow the whistle on Barney, the man she loved.

Lawler brought her into the office, gave her a cup of coffee, and tried to talk sense to her.

"Do you realize what's going on here?" he explained patiently. "Do you understand that you're the one left holding the bag?"

"I want a lawyer," she echoed Barney. "Barney said I don't have to say anything." She sat there trembling like an addict who desperately needs a fix.

"You're entitled to a lawyer," said the detective. "But if you're smart, you'll realize that the only way out of this is if you cooperate and tell us what happened."

"But I don't know," she murmured unconvincingly.

"Okay, let me lay it out for you," he said gently. "So you'll know we're not bluffing and you're looking at second-degree murder. Twenty-five to life."

Joyce shuddered and remained silent.

He spread the whole, complicated scheme before her. "The one thing we didn't realize was that it was you who followed the messengers onto the boat. Did you kill Ritter?"

Joyce went pale and it seemed that every drop of blood deserted her. She almost fell off the chair and had to grab the side of the desk to stay upright. But she still said nothing.

He was speaking softly to her now, in an almost cooing singsong. "I'm willing to bet you didn't shoot him deliberately," Lawler said coaxingly. "Your boyfriend put you in a spot where something like this could happen."

Joyce shook her head, turning away as though to avoid the terrible flood of words Lawler was raking her with.

Lawler sat back and lighted a cigarette. "We thought Barney went on the boat, but now I see he was too smart. He put your head in the noose, not his own."

She shook her head at that. "No, no," she said. "He wouldn't hurt me."

"He wouldn't, huh? He put a gun in your hand and put you in a spot where somebody could get killed."

186

"No," she said in an almost inaudible whisper.

"No? You don't realize that he set you up? You don't realize that if something went wrong, you were the one on the spot? He's tossing you to the wolves, Miss Warner. Can't you see that?"

"What do you mean?"

"I'm sure he told you nothing could go wrong, didn't he? That's what they always say. But if anything went wrong, he wasn't there. You were."

"I don't understand," she cried.

I'm sorry to say that I opened my big mouth then and said, "Joyce, don't you understand? If you don't talk, he's out of this without a scratch."

I thought Lawler was going to punch me in the head when I blurted out that little gem. The air went out of him like a spiked beach ball. "Jesus." He swallowed.

When I saw Joyce's face undergoing a transformation from cornered victim to martyred defender of the man she loved, I realized what I'd done too. "Oh, my God," I said to myself and was afraid to look at Lawler.

"That's right," she said, brightening up. "You can't touch Barney, can you?"

"Goddamn it," Lawler muttered.

"I want to make a statement," she said then. "I did it on my own. Barney tried to stop me. But I wouldn't listen."

"Aw, for the love of Christ," Lawler gasped. He glared murderously at me. "Fitzgerald, get the hell out of this office!"

I slunk out in disgrace like a kicked and extremely stupid mongrel. In the squad room sat Barney Wells with a mocking smile on his face, as certain as cast iron that Joyce would never talk. And the terrible fact was, I knew he was right. We had solved the whole tangled mess, and the guy who pulled it off couldn't be touched.

Howard Ritter's murder couldn't be pinned on him, because Joyce Warner had the gun that killed him, as a ballistics test later showed. Barney couldn't even be placed on the riverboat. There was no way to charge him with Harry Berg's murder either. Sutty did that one. Wells couldn't be placed at the Zebra Club or at Mulligan's or at Going Up on the mornings of the kidnappings. That was Ritter and then Stanley Jamison, the know-nothing messenger.

He was Ski Mask, I had no doubt. But nobody could identify him. The ransom money was still missing. I began to admire the cocky little bastard in a perverse sort of way. Two murders, three kidnappings, $70,000 lifted—very nearly $100,000.

Unless Joyce talked, he would get away with it. And Joyce's face was now radiant with the saintly demeanor of an early Christian armored in her faith. Nothing would shake her.

After a while, an assistant district attorney arrived, a reserved, suspicious-eyed young woman named Gloria Sternweiss. She was like all ADAs. She didn't want to file any charges that wouldn't stand up later in court.

She agreed to charge Joyce Warner with second-degree murder, and Jamison the messenger with possession of stolen property. That was only a formality, really, to ensure his testimony later in return for dropping the charge.

But when it came to Wells, her face went into a stubborn mask. She didn't like anything about it.

"What do you want to charge him with?" she asked a desperate Lawler. "Possession of stolen property? For two bottles of wine he found in the river?"

"Conspiracy! He set up the whole thing."

But there was no evidence, she countered. The voice print was shaky at best, and the rest was circumstantial if Joyce refused to talk.

Then Wells's lawyer showed up and demanded that Wells be charged or released. Sternweiss's face got more determined, and she shook her head.

Barney couldn't be charged with anything. When he walked out of the squad room, his mocking smile was intact.

29

THAT'S THE WAY THINGS stood a few days later at the bail hearing in Manhattan Criminal Court. I was still in disgrace. Lawler wouldn't even talk to me, and Ironhead was still screaming that I'd let the damned story blow up in my face.

When Joyce walked into the courtroom, after several days in the Women's House of Detention on Rikers Island, she looked dried out and shaky, and her face was like something I'd once seen while touring a psychiatric ward at Pilgrim State Hospital.

Assistant DA John Brother, who's squat and compact, with owlish eyes and curly hair, told Judge Long he wanted Joyce held without bail. The judge finally set $500,000 bail, which was the same thing.

The wild-eyed messenger, Stanley Jamison, was released on $300 cash bail, and went hopping out of the courtroom like a rabbit freed from a snare.

When Judge Long asked Joyce if she wanted to say anything, she only said, "No, sir." Her voice came from down a well.

Sitting out in the spectators' seats was Barney Wells, his blue shirt buttoned up for a change. He looked like the cat that got the cream, and gave me a triumphant smirk. It was certainly lovely, all right. Everybody involved in the whole damned mess was either dead or facing charges except him. I couldn't stand to look at him.

At one point he walked up to the court railing and whispered with Joyce, who kept nodding and smiling at him like a well-trained lion licking the hands of the trainer who kept it in thrall.

When it was over, Brother had some more defendants to deal with, so I walked out to the courthouse coffee shop, got some coffee, and came back out into the corridor.

Who should be standing there but Wells? He gave me a contemptuous, taunting look. "Would you like some comment for that lying rag of yours?" he said.

"Such as what?" I asked.

"Such as the nerve of you scumbags perverting the news for your own . . ."

I'm not a tough guy. Never was, never will be. But something happened when Wells went into his revolting, sanctimonious tirade. The back of my hand landed flush in his face, and blood spurted from his finely chiseled nose.

He started screeching like a eunuch! "You son-of-a-bitch! I'm bleeding! I'll have your ass!" It was hard to hear the words through the handkerchief he was stuffing into his face.

Pretty soon a uniformed court officer came walking over with a resigned look on his face. "What's the trouble?" Squabbles in the corridors were ordinary stuff to him.

"This son-of-a-bitch hit me!" Wells howled.

"He's a liar," I said quietly.

Wells face registered shock and amazement. "What?"

"Some woman slapped him," I told the court officer. "She ran out the back door."

Barney Wells's expression when confronted with this bald lie was almost comical. He couldn't believe it. "You . . . liar . . . you . . . I want him arrested!"

I looked at the court officer. "I'm a *Daily Press* reporter. You didn't see anything. You have no probable cause to arrest me. The man's lying. His girlfriend punched him out."

"Aw, shit," the officer said, and looked at Wells with a sigh. "Why don't you go fix your nose?" And he walked away.

I stood there laughing, ashamed of myself, but not sorry.

Wells slouched away, leaning against the wall and avoiding the bemused stare of a passerby. He walked to the front door, and there I saw who was waiting for him. The White Queen. They hurried out together. Sylvia Berg was clucking over him and his bloody beak.

When I got back into the courtroom, I followed John Brother, Lawler, and Joyce to the back elevator and we rode up to the ADA's office. Brother sat Joyce down across from him at his desk, studying her with his penetrating, owlish eyes.

"How are you, Joyce?" he said politely.

"Fine." But some of the starch had gone out of her on Rikers Island.

"Are you ready to talk to me?" he asked gently.

"I've already told you all there is."

John Brother slumped back in his chair and began bending a paper clip this way and that, studying it as though it held the secret of the universe. Joyce sat there stiffly, holding on.

Finally, Brother looked at her. "Why were you on pills and Scotch, Joyce?"

Joyce flushed and looked at her hands, folded in her lap. "I couldn't think about that poor man," she said. "I didn't mean to hurt him. I was only going to scare him."

"How did it happen?"

"He sat there watching me," she said. "He saw I was the only other person in the cafeteria. He called me over and asked me what I was doing there. He said, 'You know what's going on, don't you?' He said he had peeked into the bag. He said he wasn't going through with it again."

Lawler and I exchanged glances. Howard Ritter's reputation was being resurrected.

Joyce said she had walked over to Ritter, not knowing for sure what to say.

"He grabbed my arms," she said, "and held them while he

191

yelled at me. I had the gun in my right hand inside the pocket of my raincoat. I tried to push him away, and it went off."

Joyce stopped talking. The pallid mask convulsed into a spasm, and then she wept bitterly. She didn't know it then, and neither did Barney, but the scheme had crumbled at that second, when Joyce looked into Howard Ritter's face from inches away and saw death take him.

She hunched over in her chair now, reliving the shattered pinpoint in time when Howard Ritter froze and crossed over into infinity, emitting a last, severed croak. We could barely hear her through her sobs as she leaned forward, her hands over her face.

"He went, 'Uhhh!' " she said. "He swallowed his breath, and I kept waiting for him to breathe out again, but he never did. He breathed in and never breathed out again."

"After that you started taking pills?"

She nodded silently. "I couldn't sleep."

"Barney gave you those pills, didn't he?"

She said nothing.

"I know he did, Joyce. And I even know why. And when you know, you won't sit there telling us you don't want to testify against Mr. Wells."

Brother took a cloudy glass bottle with a white, snap-on top from his desk and held it up between his fingers. "These are the pills. We got them from your apartment."

"I've been looking for them."

Brother opened the bottle, and spilled them out onto his desk. "We did a lab test on them. Would you like to know what we found?"

Joyce's pale face registered confusion. "What?"

"Strychnine." He watched her face expressionlessly.

Joyce reacted with shock, dismay, rejection. She shook her head. "No," she said. "You're lying."

"Ten of them are loaded with strychnine. If you had taken one of them, you'd be dead by now. That's what Barney had arranged for you."

"No!"

"First you take the blame. Then you're dead. Case closed."

Joyce's hand flew over her mouth, and her eyes looking over them were pained and lost. She shook her head again stubbornly.

Brother nodded his head slowly, watching her. "I see," he said. "Well, maybe I'm wrong. I guess Barney couldn't have gotten away with that money. If he had the money, he would have bailed you out by now, wouldn't he?"

Another shade passed across Joyce's vision. But she held her silence.

John Brother showed nothing. "The van will be going back to Rikers," he said. "You'd better run along."

Joyce stood like one in a dream and walked stiffly out of the office.

John Brother sat there resigned. "She'll never crack now," he said. "I hit her with everything I had."

30

I T WASN'T UNTIL I was walking out of the courthouse past the spot where Barney Wells's bloodspots still stained the corridor that it finally hit me. I rode the subway back uptown to the *Daily Press* and went looking for Corky Richards, the photographer who gets those chichi pictures of soccer players and models at Studio 54. I asked him to help me out.

It took a few days, but Corky delivered the goods. Ironhead ranted and raved, but finally he even let me put the picture into the paper. Then I called Lawler and John Brother, and said I'd be down to see them.

"I'll have Joyce here," Brother said.

"If it works, I might talk to you again," said Lawler.

Buzz, the copy boy, pulled a proof of the picture page for me so I wouldn't have to wait for the Three-Star. In Brother's office in the DA's wing of the courthouse that afternoon, Joyce Warner looked institutionally faded and lethargic. The absence of pills and booze, far from bringing a healthy bloom to her cheeks, seemed to have regressed her into dullness and dowdyness. It was as though the pills and Scotch had kept her unnaturally aglow, and now only the real, wasted thing was left.

"How are you, Joyce?" John said in his gentle way.

"Fine," she said meekly.

"Are you ready to talk to us yet?"

She shook her head the tiniest fraction. "I knew you were lying. Barney wrote me."

"Hmmm," said Brother. "You know Mr. Fitzgerald from the newspaper."

She nodded hollowly. "Yes."

"He's brought you something that might interest you."

"What is it?"

"It's in the paper," Brother said. "It's about Barney."

Joyce's eyes sparkled a little and she smiled. "Barney's in the newspaper? Did he get his boat?"

"Why don't you see for yourself?" Brother put the *Daily Press* in front of her on his desk, opened to the page where the photograph was prominently displayed.

Joyce leaned over smilingly to look. Then she turned to stone. Partly bent over to gaze at the photo, she became rigid, unmoving. Her breath suddenly accelerated. Then her face flushed, she slumped forward, and a cry escaped her that I still hear in my head sometimes in the middle of the night.

With her head on the desk, she clawed the page proof and crumpled it up, shoving it off onto the floor. She was weeping brokenly. But her clawing fingers had not obliterated the picture of Barney and Sylvia Berg dancing together at a disco, jammed so closely together they were Siamese twins.

She rocked herself in the chair, keening and moaning.

"He has lots more pictures," said Brother.

And then Joyce's head jerked up. "Where?" she said violently.

I laid out the sheaf of photographs that Corky had taken of Barney and Sylvia during three days of following them around. There were enough to cover the desktop. Barney and Sylvia lunching, kissing, dancing, laughing.

Joyce examined them one by one, and her eyes weren't cloudy any more.

It took a pot of coffee, half a pack of cigarettes, and several hours for Joyce Warner to give her new statement. We were right about most of what had happened. Joyce had followed the messengers every step of the way.

"I followed them onto the boat and watched them every second," she stated. "Barney said if anything went wrong, the most I would have to do would be to scare them a little."

After the gun went off and killed Ritter, she said, she mechanically shoved the red bag over the stern, yanked the inflating cord, and dropped it. She took Ritter's walkie-talkie and slipped away to the top deck without being seen. When the boat returned to the pier, she walked off unchallenged.

I felt disgusted when I heard that. It turned out her photograph was on the police film of the people coming off the gangplank. We had been looking for a man.

Barney Wells would be parked in the rented limousine close enough to the riverboat to be able to watch Ritter and Joyce go aboard the excursion boat. Then he would leave the limousine and jump into his own car, also parked nearby.

"He drove up to the boat basin, got into his boat, and went out onto the river to wait for the excursion boat to come by," she said.

The messengers were instructed to sit in the back with the walkie-talkie and wait for Mr. Goodman to contact them from his yacht in the river. Then Ritter was told by Barney over the walkie-talkie to put everything into the red bag and throw it into the river.

It all had worked perfectly the first time. Ritter hesitated, apparently surprised at the instructions, but then followed orders. Joyce rode on to Bear Mountain and waited at the Bear Mountain Inn until Barney drove up and got her. No one could connect them with anything. "He laughed all the way back to New York."

By the end of the day, Brother had drawn up a new set of charges against Wells, including conspiracy and accessory to murder and three counts of kidnapping and extortion.

And that wasn't all. Detective Lawler got some police scuba divers to poke around in the muck of the marina under *The Boffo* and found the $70,000. That finally convinced Sylvia Berg that Barney had, indeed, taken $50,000 of her and Harry's money from the Zebra Club. She came in and gave a statement too. There was something Sylvia loved more than Barney.

Because Joyce had cooperated, she was allowed to plead guilty to involuntary manslaughter, and Brother got her out on bail to await sentencing. It looked as though she would be all right, because she probably wouldn't have to serve more than about eighteen months. But she never served a day.

One day Lawler called and told me they had just found her in her apartment, sprawled on the bed. Beside her were a Scotch bottle and a pill bottle—both empty. There was also a brief note:

"Forgive me, Barney."

Currently, Barney's on Rikers Island awaiting trial, still insisting he doesn't know anything about any of it.

As for Jennifer Ritter, she battled snooty Max Kasian and the insurance company like a tigress after her father was cleared, and finally got every penny out of them—double indemnity and all. She got over her whiplash, and today she and Angie Pinzino run J.J.'s restaurant on a converted Staten Island ferryboat in the Hudson River. I'm happy to say I never told Angie Pinzino that at one time I thought he might have been Mr. Goodman.

You may not believe this, but the idiotic New York City Police Department is still suing me and the *Daily Press* for destruction of city property. But I have no time for those things, because I'm having problems with my own insurance company.

John, who runs the service station on Second Avenue, said it will cost eighteen hundred dollars to fix the Falcon, and my insurance agent is outraged because there isn't even any listing on the book value of a 1969 Ford. He wants to give me fifty dollars for good will, but I told him I want that car put back the way it was.

"For God's sake, why?" he keeps asking me.

If you have enjoyed this mystery and would like to
receive details of other Walker mysteries,
please write to:

Mystery Editor
Walker and Company
720 Fifth Avenue
New York, New York 10019